The Unwinding Cable Car

Andrew J Brandt

Blue Handle Publishing
Amarillo

Also By Andrew J Brandt:

YOUNG ADULT
The Treehouse
The Abduction of Sarah Phillips
Palo Duro
Mixtape for the End of the World (May 2021)

ADULT NOVELS
In The Fog
Through The Fog (Nov 2021)
Picture Unavailable (May 2022)

The Unwinding Cable Car

Blue Handle Publishing
Amarillo, TX

First edition November 2020

For information about bulk, educational and other special discounts, please contact Blue Handle Publishing

Blue Handle Publishing can bring Andrew J Brandt to your live event. For more information or to book an event, contact Blue Handle Publishing.
www.bluehandlepublishing.com

Cover & Interior Design: Caprock Concepts
Editing: Brandon Biggers
Author photo: Jered Lopez

ISBN: 9781735220604

Praise for Andrew J Brandt

"[*Palo Duro*] makes me want to throw on my hiking shoes & fill up my water for a hike. You'll love the magic of the canyon Andrew J Brandt reveals."

—Niccole Caan, *KVII-TV ABC7 Amarillo*

"[*In the Fog* is] an engrossing supernatural thriller...with a dash of *Lord of the Flies* thrown in for measure."

—PenCraft Award-winning author Rick Treon

"[*The Treehouse*] is the next *Stand By Me!*"

—Dusty Boyd, *CBS Radio*

"The highlight [of *Palo Duro*] was Brandt's use of place—the scenery so evocative. The setting and the way he incorporated it into the story brought to mind the greats like Nevada Barr and Tony Hillerman. I highly recommend it!"

—Danielle Girard, *USA Today* Bestselling author

"[*In the Fog* is] the sort of story that begs to be read with a whiskey and a blanket on cold winter evenings...a welcome addition to the library."

—Derek Porterfield, author of *No-Mod*

"[*The Abduction of Sarah Phillips*] grabbed me by the collar and wouldn't let go...with some of those 'WTF' moments that I live for."

—Nicole Reeves, author of *Crimson Hearts*

"[*Palo Duro*] is a modern-day episode of *The Twilight Zone*. I couldn't put it down!"

—Mark R. Hopkins, author of *Deceit: A Life of Lies*

To Steve and Bob.

Thank you for making me believe
that I can do what you do.

For Jennifer, my real-life muse.

"Sing in me, O Muse, and through me tell the story…"
-Homer, *The Odyssey*

PROLOGUE

The day that Hamilton Raines's oldest sister Janice died started just as unremarkable as all those other late summer days in San Angelo. The humid wind that blew in from the Gulf of Mexico was sticky, and the only thing that would squelch the complaining of the Raines children was the suggestion that they all go to the backyard and play in the water sprinkler. The three children—Janice, Hamilton and Isabel—quickly stripped down into their bathing suits and were outside within just a few minutes.

Years later, his mother would admit to her surviving children, through wine-drunk tears one Christmas night, that she just wanted ten minutes of peace and quiet in the house. With three children all under the age of eight in the two bedroom home on the north side of town, those ten minutes were few and far between. No one could have predicted the horrors of that day.

The problem was with the evaporator. Called a "swamp cooler" in those parts, the machine mounted next to the house in the backyard was clunky and cantankerous and only worked when it damn well chose. It also had a short in the electrical line due to an exposed wire.

From what he recalled to the EMTs and the investigator that showed up to the house after the emergency call, Hamilton explained, though not quite understanding why Janice was slumped face-down in the mud, that she had gone to turn the water up.

As the two younger siblings ran and jumped through the oscillating stream of the sprinkler, Janice went to the knob mounted in the concrete slab of the house.

Their mother came outside through the back door just a few seconds later. "What the hell are you kids doing?" she asked, obviously perturbed. A cigarette hung from her fingers. "Who's messin' with the swamp cooler?"

The water streaming from the loose connection between the spigot and the hose formed a small pool beside the evaporator. The water met the exposed wire, and when Janice went to turn the handle on the spigot, she was met with a deadly jolt of two hundred and twenty volts. The electrocution blew the fuse in the box inside the house, which was a fortunate twist of fate. Otherwise when Mrs. Raines cradled the dead body of her oldest daughter there in the mud puddle that coalesced next to the swamp cooler, she would have been met with the same deadly electrical current.

Instead, she screamed. Hamilton could never forget that sound, piercing through the hot air, as his mother kneeled in the mud.

Mrs. June, the next door neighbor came over, seeing the desperate scene playing out through the chain-link fence that separated their properties. She whisked the two younger children back inside the house and dialed 911.

When the first responders came, Hamilton was sitting on the couch, shorts soaking into the canvas fabric of the cushions. An older man in a white Oxford shirt, the armpits stained yellow with sweat, his tie pulled to his neck loosely, kneeled next to the couch. He pulled out a small notebook from his breast pocket and asked Hamilton a couple of questions.

The seven year old boy answered quietly, his hands in his lap as he spoke. He looked down at his feet, still covered in grass clippings and mud. His butt, still wet from playing in the water, was cold against the fabric of the floral print couch.

"Hamilton? Son?"

Hamilton's little brown eyes shot up.

That is when Hamilton Raines developed the stutter.

FIRST INTERLUDE

Hamilton sat on the floor of the bedroom he shared with his remaining sister, coloring the cover of the story he'd written. The cover, stapled onto the stack of notebook paper, was a picture he drew himself. It depicted a monster appearing from a closet, which was a scene from the story.

School would start tomorrow morning, and it would be the first one that he wouldn't have Janice to walk with him.

Sitting in his bedroom, he couldn't help but dig into his school supplies, where he'd found a few sheets of loose leaf paper and wrote a story that he'd been thinking about—a boy with a magical pencil that made all his drawings come to life.

Except the boy drew monsters, and the monsters were coming for him.

There was a slight knock on his bedroom door and it opened.

"Ham, are you ready for bed?" his mother asked, leaning in the cracked doorway.

He looked up from the floor and nodded.

"What are you working on?"

"A story."

"Can I see it?" she asked.

He held the booklet aloft, the cover halfway finished. His mother knelt beside him and thumbed through it. "Did you write this yourself?" she asked.

"Y-y-y," he started, but the word wouldn't come out.

"Slow down," she said. "Think about the words you want to say."

"I wrote it b-b-by myself," he said.

"This is really good," she said, chuckling as she read the ending, where the boy was able to use the eraser end of the magical pencil to vanquish the monsters he'd unleashed into the world.

"R-r-really?"

"Absolutely. I think you could be a writer someday," his mother said.

Of the three children, he was what his teachers called *bookish*. While the girls played with dolls and their EZ Bake Oven, he was often found with a tattered *Goosebumps* book in his hands.

"It's almost time for bed," she said.

"Okay." The young boy looked up at his mother, and he could see tears begin to form in her eyes. "It's going to be okay. I am the big brother now. I'll take care of Isabel at school."

She gave him a smile that cracked through the forming sobs, and she pulled him in, holding him close. Cradling him like she did when he was much younger, she kissed him on the forehead.

"You are going to be a great writer, and a great big brother," she said.

ONE

"I've got to be honest with you, Hamilton," the man behind the onyx black desk said. He sat, reclining as far back as the chrome-and-leather chair behind the desk would go, his hands interlaced behind his head of slicked-back black hair as he looked up at the ceiling, formulating his thoughts. A gold Rolex glinted in the harsh glare from the ceiling fixtures above. "It's shit."

"Oh, come on, Brad," Hamilton argued, almost whining. "It's better than complete shit."

Hamilton Raines sat in his agent's pristine office on the sixteenth floor of the First National Bank tower in downtown Dallas, the mid-afternoon sun starting to glare through the plate glass windows that lined the west wall. The light caused little rays and rainbows to bounce around the chrome and glass surfaces and little decorations that littered the place. In a few hours, Hamilton wanted to go escape all this light, go to the streets of downtown, maybe find a bar in Deep Ellum, listen to some music from one of the local bands and get tipsy, really tipsy. Until then, he was being berated by Brad Pascal, his agent of nearly five years.

He was thankful for Brad—most of the time. The no-nonsense, tell-it-like-it-is attitude that Brad employed was one of the things that made Hamilton choose the man over the other six agents that he had his choice of when he queried his first novel. But that was three books ago and now Hamilton Raines wanted a little coddling.

"I didn't say *complete* shit," Brad said, the light playing a weird dance off his glasses. He thumbed through the manuscript, stopping every few pages to review it.

"You've got a decent idea here, I think. But, the payoff, the ending, well, it needs some work. A lot of work."

"What's wrong with the ending?" Hamilton

asked, his hands outstretched, the blazer he was wearing straining.

Endings, it turned out, were not Hamilton's strong suit. After his first novel was accepted by a big publishing house, the promotional circuit initially made him out to be the next *big thing*. The next Harlan Coben. The next Gillian Flynn. Instead, the reviews trickled in and the industry excitement soured on Hamilton Raines. Despite the sales being far below what was initially expected, Hamilton wrote two more. They didn't help, and he slowly saw less and less from each advance. The third book hadn't even out-earned the advance yet. Unfortunately, the reviews all said the same, in just a different combination of words: *Hamilton Raines's endings suck.* After all this time, all this work, his name would be just as anonymous as the countless other names on the shelves in Barnes and Noble.

The most gut-wrenching day of his life, the day Carol left nearly five months ago, was capped by making a late-night trip to the local dollar store for a gallon of milk and a bag of coffee and seeing one of his books in the bargain bin. *The bargain bin at a dollar store!*

"It's not *earned*, Ham!" Brad exclaimed, mimicking the hands-out Christ pose. "I see where you want to go with the story, but the characters need more depth before they get to the end."

"Well, what do you suggest?"

"Make them suffer," Brad said. "Readers want to feel that before the big payoff. If this is the ending you want to get to, you need your characters to *earn* it. I have to tell you, Ham, I'm getting a lot of heat from the guys in New York. We expected big sales for the last one, man. I mean, *Great Desperations* was supposed to be a monster. A *fucking monster*!"

A monster that ended up in the bargain bin. "Well, this isn't *Great Desperations*," Hamilton said with a sigh. It was true, though. That book *should* have been the monster. It was his favorite, and what he thought was his best work yet.

The New York Times, however, gave it two-and-a-half stars.

"We need to deliver a monster, though," Bad repeated the phrase, his favorite when discussing the books. A *monster* to him was the ever-elusive catch that seemed just out of grasp. "Know what I'm saying?" Brad was now leaning on his forearms on his desk, a MacBook closed and shoved to the side rested under his sleeve.

"I know, I know," Hamilton relented. He stared out the window, the taste of cheap bourbon already calling for him. "I just really thought I had it with this one."

"Well, like I said, it's not complete shit," Brad said as he flicked the corner of the pages with his thumb. The sound echoed through the office. "We've got something to work with here, at least in the first fifty thousand words. But the second half, it needs a lot of work before we even send it to the developmental editors. And I sure as shit don't want to send this manuscript to New York in the state it's in now. They'll eat us alive, Ham."

For all intents and purposes, Hamilton knew this book was it. His last shot with a big-name publisher. His contract was up after this one, and there'd been absolutely zero negotiation to renew or extend the deal for more books.

Brad looked at Hamilton with a sincere gaze. "Look, I believe in Hamilton Raines. I wanted you because I knew you had something special in you. We just haven't cracked it yet."

"Well, how do we crack it then? Because I thought this one was pretty good," Hamilton said.

"I don't know. What's your routine like right now?"

Hamilton didn't want to tell him the truth. He didn't want to tell his agent that he'd, for a lack of better term, holed himself in his apartment, sleeping during the day and drinking during the night. He'd type away a thousand words—sometimes more—before crashing on the couch. His diet at this point consisted of deli meats and white bread and cheap booze.

After all, Rolling Rock was five dollars for a six pack down at the corner store.

"My routine? I generally write at night. Try to get a thousand words on the laptop." Except a thousand words was a stretch. He'd finally been hit with the mythical dragon that all writers succumb to, the one thing that makes it all screech to a halt. Writer's block.

He'd spent days on end staring at the blinking cursor on his screen. He'd type a few words, and then delete them. He'd type new ones and just stare at them. He'd rearrange them, walk away, come back and delete everything again. The story was *there*, in his brain, but he couldn't seem to get it to flow out of his fingers and into the keyboard.

The weight of it all crashed on his shoulders as he knew that *this was it*. If he couldn't deliver on this story, he'd be out on his ass, the contract ripped up, no more advances, no more books.

"You getting out much?" Brad's voice pulled him

from his thoughts.

"Well," Hamilton stammered, chewing on the inside of his cheek. "I mean, I've been busy with this draft, and…" he trailed off.

"How's Carol?" Brad pressed.

Hamilton looked away, the memory of that worst day coming back to his mind. "She left me, Brad. You know this."

"And you've basically shut yourself up in that apartment then? I bet if I came to your place, I'd find nothing but empty beer cans and leftover sandwiches."

Right on the money. Hamilton didn't respond.

"Alright, this is what I want you to do. *Get out of the apartment*. It's nice out this time of year. I want you to find a cafe, nothing too busy, one of the local joints, and get out of the apartment and write from there," Brad said. "Some fresh air will do you some good."

"I'm not some Instagram wannabe, Brad," Hamilton scoffed. "Want me to take pictures of my coffee while I'm at it?"

"One of those Instagram wannabes just got a fifty thousand dollar advance from Grand Central Press," Brad said. "You've got a lot of potential, and I want my ten percent. So, if that's what it takes, do it."

"That's not me, though. I write thrillers, mysteries, dark shit. Not bubblegum love stories. I don't write from a cafe," Hamilton said.

"Look, just try it out. A change of scenery might be good for you."

"Write from the cafe," Hamilton sighed. He reached into his messenger bag at his feet and produced a black Leuchtturm1917 notebook. Hamilton had traditionally used it to collect his thoughts, to write down character ideas and to hash out plot points. It hadn't been cracked open in quite some time. Like a security blanket though, he kept it with him. "Might as well flash this thing around so everyone around will know that I'm a bona fide *writer*. God, I'll be a walking stereotype, with my notebook and my latte."

"Well, with some luck and some polish, this book will make you a *rich* walking stereotype," Brad said with a wink.

"Yeah," was all Hamilton could muster.

Brad Pascal chaperoned his client out the door, and a few minutes later, Hamilton was riding the elevator to the first floor of the high-rise building. Across the street, through the traffic of Fourth Street, he never noticed the little coffee shop tucked into the corner of the stone and glass building there. The metal sign above the facade read URBANA.

At one of the tables on the sidewalk outside the building, a young man sat in front of a large notebook, scribbling away with a rhythm that Hamilton recognized immediately. Dark hair falling over his brow, furrowed as he vigorously wrote, he wore all black, doing his best impression of a young Neil Gaiman. The furious scribbling without so much as looking up to sip from his iced coffee could mean only one thing—this young man, in a pair of slim-fit dark chinos and a black button-up with rolled sleeves, was *writing*.

A walking stereotype.

Checking the Kobold watch strapped to his wrist, Hamilton saw it was just after five. He figured, what the hell, he could go have a coffee and observe the atmosphere, take it in, see if it held any magic. If not, the bar in Deep Ellum was just a few blocks away.

Once the traffic cleared and he had a green cross signal, Hamilton jogged over to the coffee shop. He glanced over at the young man with the notebook and sure enough, he was writing paragraphs, dialogue.

He was writing a book.

Walking inside, the coffee shop had that roasted bean smell that was prevalent and somehow uniform amongst all the coffee shops he'd ever been in. High energy pop music swam out of ceiling-mounted speakers. A young lady in a green apron behind the counter greeted him warmly. Her purple and pink hair shone vibrantly, a physical manifestation of the hipsterness of this place.

There was no magic here, though. Nothing of this shop spoke to Hamilton Raines, or made him feel inspired. It was just a cookie-cutter coffee house, where a caffeinated hot chocolate or an iced macchiato could be had for five bucks. After perusing the menu, he ordered an iced vanilla latte, waited for it and took it back outside. With his drink in hand, he sat at one of the metal patio tables and just watched.

People were filling the streets, the rush hour beginning. Still, the young man with the notebook paid no attention to the bustle around them, sunk into his story. Hamilton envied him, envied that ability to get lost in a story as it was being written, leaking ink onto pages just to find out what happens next. As much as he loved the story, as much as he wanted—no, needed—it to be his best, to be his favorite, this last novel had been a beating, a chore. There wasn't much magic left in him. The thought of that scared him, too. He knew it as he was writing, he just didn't *feel* it like he used to. At one point in time, he could do nothing but think of his stories. In the shower, he'd come up with dialogue, acting it out with Pantene in his hair. Now, writing a book was like pulling a tooth. It was work, and it sucked. And sometimes there was blood.

The young man with the floppy hair must have felt Hamilton's eyes on him because he looked up from the open pages.

"Working on something good there?" Hamilton asked, hoping to sidestep any awkwardness.

"Oh," the man said. "Yeah, something like that."

"Are you a writer?"

"Well, kind of. I'm working on my first book," he said.

Hamilton wanted to sidle up next to him and pour five years of pessimistic wisdom in his ear. Tell him that all the book would do in the end was break his heart. No one would buy it and it would end up in a discount bin.

Instead, Hamilton smiled. "That's exciting. What's it about?"

"It's kind of a murder mystery. Three boys build a treehouse out in the woods and then discover a dead body," the man said.

"Sounds intense," Hamilton said.

"It's a story idea I've had for a long time, I just

finally feel like I have the inspiration to write it," he said.

Hamilton knew that feeling. He would do anything to get it back, to feel that excited about a book again. The unfortunate thing about work is that it eventually becomes work.

"You always write by hand?" Hamilton asked.

The young man looked down at his notebook and nodded. "Yeah, I thought I'd try it the old-fashioned way. Something about a laptop, a Word document just felt...I don't know."

Hamilton finished the sentence, "Impersonal? Like it's not real?"

"Yeah," the kid said. "Plus, Neil Gaiman writes like this, by hand. I figured I'd give it a shot too."

Bingo. Hamilton could point out the imitators a mile away.

"What's your name? That way I can say 'I ran into that guy before he was famous,'" Hamilton asked, nearly cringing at his own question. The young aspiring author lit up though.

"Well, my name is Jeremy, but I think I'll use a pen name," he said, tapping the side of his jaw with the butt end of the pen. "I was thinking J.A. Phillips."

"I like it," Hamilton said, sipping his iced coffee.

"What about you?" Jeremy "J.A." Phillips asked.

"Hamilton. Hamilton Raines," he answered.

The kid's face went flush. "What?" he finally stammered out. "Are you serious?"

Hamilton just shrugged. "In the flesh."

"Oh my god." The kid slumped back in his chair. "You're telling me I've been talking with Hamilton Raines this entire time?"

"Yeah. My agent's office is in that building," Hamilton thumbed behind him. "Thought I'd come down for a cup of coffee."

The young man shut his notebook and rummaged through a canvas backpack at his feet. He produced a copy of *Great Desperations*. "This is my third time reading it," he said, cradling it in his hands like a precious object. "It's literally my favorite book of all time." Then he looked up at Hamilton, hopeful yet embarrassed to ask, though Hamilton knew what question was coming.

"Will you sign it for me?"

Hamilton smiled. "Of course I will." That was still his favorite part of writing. Despite how much the process and the business of it seemed to have drained him over the last five years since his first novel, he never tired of signing autographs.

Phillips got up from his table and crossed the patio to Hamilton, who pulled a Waterman fountain pen from the inside of his jacket. Taking the book from the kid's hands, he felt the spine, the bent and broken corners, the way the pages fanned even when lying flat. The book had been well-loved. He cracked it open to the title page and scrawled his name in blue Waterman ink that flowed from the pen. Underneath, he wrote the inscription, "To J.A. Phillips, from your first fan."

He handed the book back to the kid who beamed at the autograph.

"This is seriously the best day of my life," he said.

Though Hamilton didn't hear him. His attention was suddenly and completely drawn elsewhere.

Walking up the sidewalk and into the front doors of Urbana was a woman unlike any he'd ever seen in his life. Of course he'd seen beautiful women, had a few notches on the bedpost, but this woman in front of him seemingly glowed in a halo of light and beauty. Her long brown hair fell in ringlets that framed a perfectly round face. Her lips, plump and red, juxtaposed the cream color of her skin. Hamilton blinked once, twice, perhaps to shake himself from this enraptured seizure of his attention.

She looked at him, smiled, bright white teeth glinting in the happy hour sun and as she walked inside, no longer in his line of sight, the spell broke.

The kid's voice brought him back to reality. "Anyway, thank you so much for this. It means the world to me."

He looked up at the kid, who was still admiring the autographed page in his copy of *Great Desperations*.

"Oh," Hamilton said. "Yeah, kid. Anytime."

Grabbing his backpack, Phillips tossed both the newly-autographed book and his notebook in its large cavity. "Thank you again," he said. "Maybe I'll see you around here again sometime?"

"Yeah, maybe." *Probably not.*

Hamilton got up to leave as well. He threw his drink, which was just water and ice stained with milk at this point, into the trashcan by the tables. It was time to head back home. He turned to the sidewalk and nearly ran face-first into the beautiful woman, who had come out the door.

"Oh my goodness," she said, startled, juggling the drink in her hand so that it didn't slosh all over the both of them. "I am so sorry." Her voice was tinged with a hint of an accent that Hamilton couldn't immediately place. Mediterranean, maybe?

"No, no, it's my fault," Hamilton said. "I wasn't watching where I was going."

Up close, she was even more beautiful. Not just

beautiful—flawless. If he were to build his dream woman, she would look something like her.

"Do you know him?" she asked, nodding toward Phillips who was now a block down the sidewalk, waiting for a crossing signal to change.

Hamilton turned. "Oh, that kid? No. I just met him. Why?"

"I see him here often," she said. "He is a writer. I thought maybe you were a friend of his."

"No. I just found this place." He was about to explain that he was a writer as well, that his agent had suggested he find a coffee house like this, but he didn't want to come off as cocky. Instead, he said, "I need to get going myself. Enjoy your coffee."

"Well, I hope to run into you again soon," she said.

Hamilton didn't know how to respond. It sounded flirty, and he liked it. The way she spoke, it made him feel like he still *had it.* "I hope so," he finally said.

Walking to the DART station that would take him back home, he couldn't help but let his mind wander, to let his imagination come up with every sort of scenario involving this beautiful woman. It felt crazy, but he absolutely wanted to see her again.

TWO

Hamilton woke up the next morning to the sun filtering through the open window curtains, which bathed the loft apartment in a light that it hadn't seen in months. The rush of cars on the streets below the loft rumbled that regular hum of morning that he'd become accustomed to living in the city. In the past, he always thought he'd be the type of writer that would live somewhere in the sticks, far away from civilization and people, like a modern-day Walden. Instead, he'd come to love the hustle and bustle of the city.

It also didn't hurt that there was a half-dozen bars within walking distance.

His eyes blinked open and his body demanded

coffee. He looked at the clock on his nightstand, the red LCD letters reading just before nine. He decided to get up, take a shower, and do what Brad had suggested—write from a coffee shop. The young man, J.A. Phillips, had inspired him, in a weird circle of artistic expressiveness. Maybe Brad was right—maybe a change of scenery was exactly what he needed. Maybe he'd been so caught up in his rut that he'd forgotten the first rule of writing—to write, you must first *live*. In simpler terms, it's hard to write what you know if all you know is naps, beer and cold cut sandwiches.

He got out of bed and stretched his joints. Looking around the bedroom, he realized something was missing—all the clutter, trash, dirty clothes, all of it was gone. He didn't even remember cleaning up. It looked like a brand new apartment, sparkling in this window-filtered morning light. Even the nightstand, usually littered with empty cups, discarded Hostess wrappers and other trash, was not only completely cleared, but also dusted.

Now that he was awake and conscious, his body felt completely rested and relaxed. The initial demand for coffee was more a habit than anything else. Nonetheless, Hamilton was going to shower, shave and take the DART train downtown, to the coffee shop across from the First National Bank tower. Even though Brad had suggested a quieter local place, his mind was dead set on going back to that cafe on the corner.

Like the young aspiring author he had met and signed a book for, he'd take his notebook and his laptop and sit at one of the metal patio tables and begin writing.

Not *working*. His mind didn't even think of it as work. No, he was ready to create, to mold a story, to coax words onto paper. On his dresser, the marked-up manuscript that his agent had disparaged and disregarded as "not *complete* shit" sat, taunting him. Hamilton's first instinct was to chuck it in the trash, but perhaps there really was something in its pages, some hidden gem buried in the dirt that he just needed to extract.

Thirty minutes later, he was showered, cleaned up and dressed. He wore a pair of khakis and a white button-up kept untucked and the sleeves rolled up. His glasses, chunky black frames, were tucked in the front pocket and he gathered up the manuscript, his laptop and his Lamy pen. Opening his bedroom door to the living room, he gasped.

It looked even better than the bedroom. All the once-cluttered surfaces were cleaned and cleared of disorder. The kitchen countertops damn near *sparkled.*

His normally internal monologue blurted out of his mouth, unable to be contained. "What the hell did I do last night?"

You cleaned up, his brain answered.

The ferns by the door that led to the patio looked perked up. Even the trashcan tucked beside the kitchen bar had a new bag in it.

The entire apartment looked amazing. It glowed. Glowed like…

His brain went to the woman, replaying the scene on the patio of the coffee shop yesterday. He could only think about how she too had glowed in that late afternoon sun.

It felt ridiculous, but also plausible. That perhaps, just maybe, if he went to write there today, she would show up again.

Hamilton pushed the thought away. It was ludicrous.

Still, he gathered up his things and went to grab his messenger bag, but it wasn't lying on the floor by the door in its customary spot. Now he panicked. Where, if he'd cleaned this entire apartment the night before, would he have put the bag? He opened the coat closet by the front door and found it hanging on a peg, beside his sportscoats and blazers, all not only hung on the rack, but in ascending colors — from grey to brown to black.

What the… his brain started.

He just shrugged, thanking himself for this strange turn of events and, tucking his computer and notebook into the bag, walked out the door and down to the street level. The DART station was just a few blocks away and the morning air was gorgeous, a few puffy clouds above cutting little shapes in the cerulean sky. He arrived just in time for a departure to downtown proper, the skyscrapers of Dallas just a few miles ahead in the distance. Deep Ellum, the old warehouse district that Hamilton called home, was across the highway and the home to many artist types.

After his first novel was picked up by the publishing house in New York, he and Carol had bought the flat above an old warehouse in the district. Not only did they think it would be an inspiring place to live, he was able to reconnect with a part of his life that he thought he'd left behind when they'd graduated from the University of North Texas—the music scene. At night, the bars would be full and music could be heard from their depths. In the morning though, Deep Ellum was a ghost town. Ghosts, after all, only come out at night.

He boarded the DART at the station, paid his fare and took the train, where he was deposited at the feet of the tall metal and glass office buildings. From the station it was just a four block walk to Urbana on the corner of Fourth Street. The sun was already high in the morning sky, but as Hamilton strode along the sidewalks, he hoped that he hadn't missed the rush of cafe dwellers. Because he wanted to see *her* again.

Hamilton brought himself back to reality, shaking his head. It was madness, even as his feet continued despite his brain's protests. Maybe there was just something magical about that corner cafe, despite his initial doubts.

Outside of the coffee shop, the tables were in place, black metal squares on pedestals. A man sat at one, talking on his cell phone. At another, two women were engaged in close conversation, their laughter occasionally breaking through the din of the street. Hamilton took one for himself, setting his bag on the table and extracting his laptop. Powering the device on, he opened up the Word file of his current manuscript and began working.

The first thing to do was to read it through, making highlights where Brad had marked up the paper copy. Something told him, though, to just scrap it, to start fresh. Though Brad did say that the first fifty thousand words were decent, he knew he could do better than decent. He wanted the monster. And what he had now just wouldn't cut it.

It was the ending.

Endings always gave Hamilton fits.

He opened a second Word file and copied the first twelve chapters of his book to it. He'd start fresh, from chapter thirteen on. A clean slate, with a diving board. He read through the twenty pages leading up to it, his protagonist—a private investigator on the tail of a suspected cop killer—discovering new clues to solve the case. So, with a blank page and a blinking cursor, he prepared himself to start writing.

Except, nothing was coming out.

He had felt so sure of himself, so sure that this place held the magic, the stuff. Except this cafe, where J.A. Phillips, Hamilton Raines superfan, chose to write, just wasn't doing it.

Hamilton felt stupid. This whole idea was stupid. He reached up to shut the laptop lid and saw her. There she was, as if she had materialized out of thin air, magically sitting at the table no more than three meters from him. She held a book in her hand, the paperback folded over itself. It looked massive, not like a dollar store pulp.

Not *Great Desperations*.

He gulped, felt the blood flush his cheeks.

She looked up as if the sound in his throat alarmed her and caught his gaze. Hamilton quickly looked away and, pushing his glasses up on the bridge of his nose, put his attention back on the screen. Placing his fingers on the keys, he took a breath.

And the words flowed.

Some faucet inside his body opened, a gush of thoughts all at once and his fingers could barely keep up. He glanced up occasionally to see that she still sat, reading her book, lazily turning the pages. Every time he stole a glance her way, she would look up as well. On the third time, she smiled at him.

On the fourth time, she got up.

Hamilton felt so foolish. *She thinks you're a creep*, he thought.

She didn't walk away though. Instead, to his dread and surprise, she walked to his table.

"I think we were having a staring contest," she said in her accented voice.

"N-n-no," he stammered. The stutter caught him off guard. He hadn't done that since he was a young child. The words *I'm sorry* and *you're right* all came out at once and he said, "I'm right you're sorry."

She looked at him quizzically and Hamilton shook

his head. He collected himself and then said, "You're right. I think we were. Would you like to sit?" he gestured to the open chair across the table.

"You looked busy with your work. I didn't want to bother you," she said. "I'm going to grab a tea. Would you like anything?"

He declined and as she walked into the cafe, he couldn't help his eyes as they followed her all the way to the door.

As she was inside, he looked at the Word document and did a word count search to see that he'd written over two thousand words in the hour and change that he'd been there. Most of the time he was lucky to get five hundred—a grand on a really, really good day. Here, he'd broken through and it all had fallen out onto the keyboard almost effortlessly, like it had in the old days, writing his first novel.

He felt that excitement, that nervous jitter in his legs, that he always felt when he knew he was creating something good. Putting his fingers back down on the keyboard, he continued typing, not stopping to edit, not stopping to read, just getting the story out.

That's the secret, he told himself. *Write fast and don't stop until the story is out.*

Hamilton felt, more than heard, the door of the cafe open. The gorgeous woman came back out, a plastic cup in each hand.

"I decided to get you something," she said. "It's my favorite. Iced chai latte."

Hamilton took it from her outstretched hand and thanked her. "That's very sweet of you," he said. "You didn't roofie it, did you?"

She laughed and sat across from him. "No, nothing like that. I just thought you would like it. You seem to be in deep concentration."

"Oh, I'm just working on something," he said.

She smiled. "Are you a writer?"

"Is it really that obvious?"

"I can usually pick them up. I admittedly have a thing for writers," she said, flashing a smile from her red lips and perfect white teeth.

Hamilton reached across the table to offer his hand. She took it and shook with a grip that was both feminine yet strong.

"I'm Hamilton Raines," he said.

"I am Calliope," she said in return.

Fitting, he thought. "Like the muse?"

"Something like that," she said. Again, that smile. And again, it melted Hamilton a little.

"Your accent?" he inquired. "Where are you from?"

"Europe," she said. "Near the Mediterranean."

"I thought so," he said. "It's gorgeous."

"Thank you," she said. "What are you writing?"

"Oh, nothing serious. Just my next book. I write thriller novels, mysteries," he answered.

"Ooh," she cooed. "I like mysteries."

"Well, hopefully a lot of other people do too and this one actually sells." He took a sip of the iced chai, mimicking Calliope as she did the same. It tasted delicious on his tongue, hints of vanilla and spices swirling in the sweetness. "Wow, that's really good," he said.

"Like I said, it's my favorite."

Hamilton nodded to her book, which she'd placed face-down on the table. "What are you reading?"

"The Odyssey," she said, picking it up and showing him the cover.

It was a very old book, he could tell, and this copy had been read and loved for many years. He hadn't read the story since he was in high school. The coincidence of her name wasn't lost on him, however.

"You know, Calliope the muse is said to have inspired Homer to write his epics," he said, trying to sound educated. Hoping, perhaps, that his knowledge would impress this woman.

She, however, gave him a smirk. "Are you—oh,

goodness, what is the word? My English is not perfect. Are you explaining it like a man?"

"Am I mansplaining?" he asked, guiltily.

"Yes, that is the word."

"N-n-no," he stammered again. He felt like an idiot for at least the half-dozenth time already today, but the woman laughed at his blushing.

"I am kidding you," she said, and sipped her iced chai. She picked up the book and admired the cover, depicting Odysseus and his men on a ship in a storm. "This is one of my favorite stories. Every time I read it, I find something new to cherish."

He loved that answer. "The best stories do that, don't they?"

"Yes, and this is one of the best."

Hamilton looked at his own work, hoping that someday someone would gush about his stories like that.

"Do you come here often?" she asked him.

He looked back up at her. "Actually, this is my first time. Well, second, actually. Sorry. I was here yesterday afternoon," he said. "But you know that." *God, get it together, Hamilton.* "For a few minutes. Just wanted to check it out."

"That other writer here yesterday, you were sitting with him?"

"Well, he and I weren't together yesterday. I just happened to come by while he was working on a novel."

"He asked for your autograph," she said, matter-of-factly. "I saw you from the window, signing his book. You must be famous for people to ask for your autograph."

"I wouldn't say I'm famous, but it is nice to be known. To be recognized," he said.

"Do you want to be famous?" she asked, a curious look in her eyes.

"I don't know, honestly," he said. "I'd like to be known for my works, to be able to make a good living doing this, but is fame tied to fortune? Can you have one without the other?"

"These are good questions, asked even in the times of Homer," she answered. "And all I can say is, if you do your best, if people appreciate the art you create, then you should welcome the fame that comes with it. People still know who Homer was. People still study Shakespeare."

Hamilton nodded and sipped again.

She looked at the watch on her wrist and stood from the table. "I am sorry I must go so quickly, but I have a meeting scheduled soon that I must attend."

Hamilton stood and shook Calliope's hand.

"Well, I will be here, working," he said. "Tomorrow as well. I'd love to see you again."

"I will make it a point to see you again. Same time tomorrow?" she asked.

He nodded yes.

It was a date.

THREE

Hamilton worked from that corner cafe nearly every single day for a month. Like clockwork, he would wake up early to the sounds of morning traffic outside his apartment on the streets below. Before this new habit, his blasé ambivalence would mean a nap before noon, perhaps he would bang out a few hundred words—if he was lucky—and he would nap again. He'd find himself drunk on bourbon before crashing on the bed or the couch and wake up to do it again the next day. If he were smarter, he would have bought stock in Tylenol and Gatorade.

This new routine was more than just that, though. It was a reignition in his belly, a fire that he'd not felt in a long time. On some mornings, after his trek to the downtown coffee shop, Calliope would join him at his self-assigned table and when she spoke, it was like dripping knowledge and inspiration directly into his brain. Sometimes she wouldn't show, and the words would still come, even if more labored. But still, he worked on his manuscript. Almost blindly, almost as if the words themselves took on a life whether he paid attention to them or not, they would fall from his fingertips, the *clack clack clack* of the MacBook keyboard the score to the burgeoning story.

Hamilton couldn't even tell you when he went to bed at night, when he stopped writing, stopped thinking, but the next morning he would wake up just as he had done the morning before, well-rested and welcoming in the morning light.

It felt like coming out of hibernation after a season tucked away out of the cold. Perhaps that's exactly what it was. And, really, Hamilton was glad for it. In the light of this new day and this new excitement for his work — and, to be honest, Calliope, though he tried not to think about her too much because it made him feel childish, like a schoolboy crush — he was happy to get back to work.

His career, after all, was on the line.

He found a pair of khakis—hanging smartly on a

hanger in the closet, the rest of his pants in order from light to dark— and another button-up shirt, this time white instead of blue. It felt good to get dressed, to forgo the sweatpants and the t-shirts for something that made him feel sexy.

He brushed his teeth, pulled on a pair of brown Chelsea boots to finish his outfit for the day, and was out the door headed for the station. This new routine, even after a month, was invigorating. The morning sunshine felt great, and it wasn't too late in the season where the sun began its torrential beating early in the day; no, these mornings were comfortably warm, perfect for sitting outside and writing.

He'd usually written the entirety of his novels from a table tucked away in the apartment, far from any distractions. That, he always thought, was the secret. In order to create something worth reading, he needed to be somewhere he didn't necessarily want to be, without any distractions or windows looking out to a world that would invariably attempt to entice him to come out, to abandon the project for *just one day*. Because he knew, as most writers did, that the routine was king, and if you gave up one day, you gave up a month. He'd shuddered when Brad suggested writing from the cafe because it was a *change*. Change is terrible for routine, but maybe, Hamilton now thought, with his perfectly unwrinkled pants and brown boots that seemed to fit better than ever and his apartment uncluttered, that this change was exactly what he needed.

And Calliope…

Something about that woman kept her right there in the crevices of his brain, never fully leaving, but staying just within grasp of the next daydream. He would close his eyes just to remember what she looked like. He would replay entire conversations in his head, dissecting each word she said. Their conversations looped in his mind as he remembered her brunette locks that framed that perfectly round face and heart-shaped lips.

He hadn't even so much as looked at a woman in months. Hadn't dared think that he could even want someone again, the company, the laughter, the infatuation. But here it was, and he welcomed it openly.

After the DART ride downtown, Hamilton walked to the coffee shop, plopped his messenger bag on the table and pulled out his MacBook. Opening the computer, he clicked the file, the *second draft*, and stared at it in disbelief.

He did some math in his head and double-checked the word count on the file again, because there was no way it was accurate. According to the screen and the running word count at the bottom of the window, he'd written six thousand words yesterday. That was the most he'd ever written in one sitting, and for a moment he just sat back in the chair, and admired the word count. He was *back.*

It seemed like a large number for the amount of time he'd sat outside Urbana and he didn't remember writing any more in the evening yesterday. Though, he reminded himself, he also didn't remember doing things like folding his sweatpants or organizing his closet or cleaning the entire apartment.

Perhaps, he figured, he was in *the zone*, this mythical mindset where the story just flowed without thought, that he'd successfully cracked through the lethargy and depression of Carol's absence. That *this* was what normal felt like, not the wringing each word from his consciousness with almost brute force, but allowing it to just...*flow.*

Whatever it was, Hamilton Raines liked it.

He began to type, but first he read through what he'd written the day before. And he *loved* it. Not in the way that he loved all his works, but he genuinely was excited by the way the words flowed, the syntax and diction. The prose, while not pretentious, was gorgeous. There was no chance Brad would call this *complete shit.*

Typing away at the screen, he also kept his attention around him, hoping that Calliope would show up at any moment. He kept the chair opposite from him empty and inviting. Until she showed up, he got to work. The story was taking a new direction he'd never anticipated, but getting to see the overarching plot with new eyes helped with the fresh direction. It no longer felt stale, this whole process.

Hamilton had never been one to plot out his stories anyway. He wrote, borrowing a euphemism, by the seat of his pants. His stories generally started out with a what-if scenario, a character idea, and then written to see—even for himself—what happened to those characters in that scenario. Sometimes it worked. Sometimes it was apparent that he would need to do a lot of revising when he went back to read that first draft. Character's names would sometimes suddenly change in the middle of the manuscript.

Sometimes it really was *complete shit.*

Not this time, however. Hamilton genuinely *liked* what he'd written on these pages, even if he couldn't specifically remember writing it. It all just felt inspired and fresh.

"Hello Hamilton."

The voice broke his concentration but he knew who it was before his brain had even registered it. He looked up from the computer screen, and Calliope was there, sitting across from him, resplendent as ever. How he never noticed her until that moment evaded him, except for the idea that he'd simply been completely immersed in the task at hand.

She already had two iced chai lattes on the table.

"I was beginning to think you weren't coming here anymore," he said. It had been five weeks since their first conversation, but now that she was here, he was bursting with excitement. "I could definitely get used to this," Hamilton said. He took one of the drinks that she pushed toward him.

"How is the writing?" she asked.

"It's," he paused, collecting himself so that he wouldn't devolve into a stuttering mess. "It's great, actually. Better than I could have expected."

"This is good," she said. She smiled, a look on her face that he could have taken as pride.

"I'm glad you came again today," he said. "I think you are my good luck charm."

"Oh?" she asked.

"Ever since we met , this story has really taken shape and I am really liking how it's coming together. I was afraid that I'd written myself into a corner, but I found a new direction for it."

"Well, I will be your good luck charm then."

"In fact, with your name, I would even say you're my muse."

She didn't say anything in response to this, just smiled coyly as her lips wrapped around the straw of her drink. Finally, she asked, "How long have you been a writer?"

"Goodness," Hamilton said as he leaned back in his chair. The truthful answer was, *as long as I can remember*. He hated that answer because it implied that somehow writers were born with this innate ability to form words into sentences, into paragraphs, into chapters, into books. To tell a story was universal, but it took dedication to the craft, a learned skill. Any Tom, Dick or Harry—with enough time and enough dedication—could sit down and write a novel eventually, just as anyone could learn, with enough training and education, how to wire a house or build a coffee table. It took time and effort, not necessarily some arbitrary gene that flipped on or off at birth.

"My first book was published five years ago, but I guess I've always had stories in my head. When I was younger, they were just poor imitations of the books I'd grown up reading. But, the short answer is, as long as I can remember." Hamilton took a sip of the latte that she'd brought him. It tasted sweeter yet more delicious than the first one she'd given him that first time he'd come to write here. "These are great," he said, nodding to the cup. "How long have you lived in Dallas?"

"I have not been in this city very long. I am fairly new. But places like this are universal. They attract the same type of people no matter where you are in the world, and I like that. I can find my people here," she said. Glancing at the watch on her wrist, the dial attached with a woven gold band, Calliope stood from the table. "I must be going now."

Hamilton stood as well. "I'm so glad I got to see you again," he said. "This needs to become a regular thing." He motioned to the tabletop. "I like these little coffee shop meetings."

She gave him a warm smile that made him weak in the knees. "Yes, I will see you here again."

The woman offered her hand and he shook it. As she began to walk away, Hamilton's eyes were glued on her backside. He ran over to the railing that separated the cafe's patio from the rest of the sidewalk.

"Hey, Calliope!" he called out. She turned back to him, already several yards away. She walked back over.

"Yes?"

"Would you like to have drinks with me tomorrow evening? There's a new bar in my neighborhood that

I've been wanting to check out and one of my friends from college is playing a gig." The statement was actually a lie. The bar was new, the latest venture from Corby, his roommate from college. Hamilton had very little desire to *check it out* until this very moment. The idea sprung in his mind without warning. Hamilton needed the reassurance that he'd see her again, and even more so, he wanted to show her off to his friends. *I'm thriving.*

"I think I would like that," she said.

"Great," he said. "Meet me at the Deep Ellum DART station at eight o'clock?"

She smiled. "I will see you there." Then, she reached over the barrier and pulled him into a hug. Hamilton could have stayed there all day. Her perfume, honey and lavender, wafted through his nostrils and all his senses tingled.

Calliope let go and then turned once again and made her way down the sidewalk, the red-soled shoes she wore disappearing into the sea of people.

Hamilton just stood there, his body already craving her touch again. After a moment that lasted all morning, he went back to the table and sat in front of the computer screen. He began typing, and didn't stop until he realized the sidewalks and streets were full of people leaving their offices for the day. He looked down at the word count at the bottom of his screen.

He'd typed nearly ten thousand words.

FOUR

Whether it was the influence of his new infatuation, or just the difference in environment, Hamilton had never felt more confident in his life, more at peace with life. A part of him wanted to call up Brad or even send the man a fruit basket. *Thanks for the tip, it changed my life.* This entire routine had not only changed his writing, made him more excited to work than he had in years, it also made him, dare he say, glow. In the mirror, brushing his teeth, Hamilton realized that he was actually smiling as he did so.

Even though he was scheduled to see Calliope tonight, he decided to go to the cafe this morning anyway. He wanted to not only to get a few words in, but perhaps, if he was lucky, he'd run into the woman again, a little preamble to their scheduled meeting tonight.

He got dressed and gathered his writing tools. Before he left the apartment, he checked himself in the mirror once again.

"Lookin' good," he said to his reflection. "Lookin' good." The words slid off his tongue in a sly smoothness that sounded like they belonged to someone else.

Taking the stairs from his loft to the street level, Hamilton rode the DART and was at the cafe within thirty minutes.

The barista, the same girl with the purple and pink hair, greeted him with a smile. "Good morning, Mr. Raines," the young woman said.

"Good morning," he replied cheerfully.

"Would you like your usual? Iced chai, correct?" the barista, her name tag reading *Skye*, said.

"Um," he stammered. "Yes. That's it." Usually, it was Calliope who ordered the iced chai for him, but perhaps the barista remembered that Calliope would always order two—one for herself and one for the writer.

She rang it up and took his payment. "Working on anything good?" she asked.

"Well, we'll see how good it is when it's published,

but I am excited for the story," he said. "Are you a reader?"

"Absolutely," she said. "But I do have a question." Skye the barista handed him his change. "You left a lot of things unanswered at the end of *Great Desperations*. Does that mean we are getting a sequel?"

"I always thought that the questions were left open because they weren't important. What was important was the experience of the characters, despite the world changing around them," he said. "But, if I get enough requests for a sequel, I bet there's one in me."

This kind of recognition was alien, but Hamilton welcomed it. These little moments added up. Between Jeremy Phillips asking for an autograph and now the barista, for the first time in his career as a writer, it felt real. He felt like more than someone toiling over a Word document.

He hung around the bar for a few minutes as his drink was crafted and the barista handed it to him. "Thank you, Mr. Raines," she said. "It's always nice to see you here."

Taking the drink outside, he sat at his customary table and opened his laptop. The amount of words he'd produced just in the last month was amazing, but more than that, it was the *quality* that dumbfounded him. He wanted to kick himself in the ass, that he hadn't done this a long time ago. He never realized how deep in the rut he'd been. Like the frog in the boiling pot, sometimes it's too late and you're floating at the surface, never realizing you were dying the entire time.

He began to type, but the words today didn't flow as freely as he'd like. They came in spurts, a few sentences here, a paragraph there. After an hour, he checked the word count at the bottom of the screen and was pleasantly surprised to see that the ticker had gone up by another thousand. At this rate, he'd have something to turn into Brad by the end of the month. Boy, would that be a surprise.

While he wrote, Hamilton kept one eye focused on his periphery, hoping to see her walk up the sidewalk. A couple of times he thought he caught a whiff of honey and lavender and his head darted back and forth, but he never saw Calliope and her flowing caramel macchiato hair. He would see her this evening though, he reminded himself. *Just work on this manuscript to pass the time and then she's yours all night.* It sounded presumptuous, though he completely believed it at the same time.

After another hour, he got up from the table,

packed away his computer and notebook into his bag and started toward the DART station to go back to the apartment. He'd grab a late lunch, answer emails and get ready for his date tonight.

As he started down Fourth to the station, he heard a sound behind him, a scuffling of feet on the concrete. Then, a voice, "Hey, you! Hey, asshole!"

Hamilton turned and he saw the rage and anger before he saw the man. In a second, he was on Hamilton, nearly shoving him into the wall. It was Jeremy Phillips.

"Who the hell do you think you are?" Phillips asked Hamilton.

"Whoa, whoa, whoa." Hamilton held his hands up, trying to diffuse the situation while also simultaneously attempting to figure out what the kid was railing about. When they'd first met, after that disastrous meeting in Brad's office, the young man was gushing about Hamilton's books, and they hadn't seen each other since. "What's going on? What's wrong?"

"You," Phillips spat, his dark hair in shambles, wiry curls spewing in every direction. He looked like he hadn't slept since that day outside Urbana. Dark circles ringed his eyes, which sunk into his skull. His facial hair, perfectly manicured into a short stubble when they'd first met, was unruly now, specked with dirt and fifth. His dark outfit looked disheveled and frayed. "You're what's wrong. You took her from me."

"Took her from you? Took who?" This behavior seemed familiar to Hamilton. He'd seen this type of thing before, when he was younger. Guys in college tweaking out on Adderall and pacing the halls of the dorms, their eyes framed in dark circles and mumbling things that flowed from an unfiltered brain.

"*You know who*," Phillips began pacing now, his steps repeating the same meter over and over. He clutched at his hair. "You stole her!" he yelled.

"Kid," Hamilton said, "just calm down." And then it clicked. *Calliope*. Was the young aspiring writer infatuated with her as well? Did she meet Phillips for coffee before he'd met her?

"You listen to me right now." Jeremy Phillips stopped pacing, a moment of clarity breaking through. "Just because you're some big shot writer with a publisher and an agent and all that *bullshit* doesn't mean you can just throw your weight around and take whatever you want. She's *mine*, you hear me? She's *my* muse."

"Look, I'm not taking anything from you. Are you talking about Calliope?" Hamilton asked and the kid shuddered a nod. "She's a big girl. She can see whomever she wants. And I'll tell you this," Hamilton looked him up and down, "she isn't going to want someone acting a fool like this. Go home, Phillips. Get some sleep. And take a shower, for Christ's sake."

Unable to contain it anymore, Phillips fell to his knees, bawling, clawing at his eyes. His wails pierced through the din of traffic and construction around them. Hamilton shoved himself past the crazed young man. "I don't have time for this shit," he said haughtily. It was a phrase that his father had used often, and the words came out in a gruff voice that he didn't recognize as his own.

As he walked off, his pace quick, hoping that he hadn't missed the DART to Deep Ellum, Hamilton couldn't help but wonder if the woman with whom he was so infatuated was pulling this young man along as well. They did, after all, frequent the same coffee shop.

Hamilton shoved the thought away. It was clear that the kid was just one of the crazies, the overzealous type that freaked out when things didn't go his way. And so what if Calliope chose to spend time with him? There was no law that she couldn't. The presumptuousness of the young man—*she's mine*—

was disgusting.

However, in the back of his brain, tucked beneath all sense and sensibility was a tiny thought.

No. She's mine.

FIVE

He wore a black Henley with the sleeves pulled up over his forearms and a pair of dark jeans and black laced boots. He found himself pacing, tapping his feet on the asphalt. There was the thought that maybe she had stood him up. All that pent-up nervousness melted away when he saw her emerge from the DART.

Hamilton's knees went weak. There she was, that dark brown hair falling in layers over her shoulders. The black dress she wore was simple yet sexy as it molded to the curves of her hips. The front was cut low, a hint of cleavage poking out. She saw him and smiled.

"I hoped I was at the right place," Calliope said. "I almost got off on the last stop." She reached for him and hugged him and he couldn't help but hold on for a heartbeat longer than necessary.

"You look amazing," Hamilton said as he pulled himself away.

"As do you," she said, that smile never ceasing.

"Where are we going?" she asked.

"Club Gaga, over on Elm. Not too far from here," he answered, unable to peel his eyes from her.

They began walking as he told her about the new bar. He explained how Corby, who was his oldest friend and college roommate, was opening the place in a rebuilt warehouse with tonight as the soft opening. The band on the bill, a retro rock band in the Radiohead style, was fronted by a mutual friend from college, Dan Paul Bailey. They'd all lived in the dorms together at the University of North Texas back in the early-aughts. "I love live music," he said. "It's art at its most raw."

"I like that. I will have to remember it."

"You know," Hamilton said. He turned to her as they walked side by side. "I never got your last name."

She chuckled. "It's okay. It's a Greek name. It's

Angelos."

The irony wasn't lost on Hamilton. *Calliope the angel.*

"So, something very strange happened earlier today," he said. "And, I just wanted to know if you knew anything about it. Do you know Jeremy Phillips? Goes by J.A.?"

Her eyes turned to him, wide with surprise and she stopped in her tracks. "Oh no," she said.

"Oh no, what?" he asked. "It's okay if you're seeing him. We're not exclusive here. But he was..." Hamilton paused, trying to describe the young man's breakdown. "Agitated."

"He is obsessed with me," she said.

"I can see that."

She continued, "I met him a few months ago, and we hung out a few times. He's a writer, like you. Except," she looked Hamilton up and down, "not like you. He wants to be like you."

Hamilton nodded. He had picked up on that.

"He was very upset, saying that you are *his*," Hamilton shrugged. "He was convinced, insanely, that you had left him for me."

Calliope turned to him, stopping her tracks. "I do not care what he believes, and I'd prefer not to talk about it any further," she said curtly.

Hamilton nodded with understanding. "I get it. Some men can be...weird." Perhaps this young man was stalking her, making her life hell. Crazier stories abounded, and if this was one she didn't want to talk about, then he would respect that.

She doesn't want to talk about him because she chose you, the voice in his head said.

"Weird, yes. But not you. You are not weird." She smiled and again, Hamilton's stomach did somersaults.

They arrived at the bar, the lights outside illuminating the marquee that read **CLUB GAGA OPENING NIGHT AUDIOSMITH.** There was a crowd at the door, paying the cover charge to get in and Hamilton led Calliope to the front of the line.

"Hey, Jason," Hamilton said to the doorman, a burly mountain of a man with a red beard that hung down to his chest.

"What's going on, Ham?" Jason asked. "Good to see you tonight. I know Dan Paul and his guys will be happy you're here. Add some legitimacy to the joint."

"You're too kind," Hamilton said.

Jason pulled back the red rope that barred the entrance and let Hamilton and Calliope in.

"Do you know everyone down here?" she asked as

they walked through a dimly lit entryway that opened into the large concert hall. The former warehouse, fitted with a bar near the back of the room which already buzzed with people, was gutted into a space large enough to fit a thousand people, with a stage at the far end. The stage was already set with lights already flickering and a projector screen with the Audiosmith logo illuminated.

"I just happen to know a lot of the guys in the music scene down here. We all grew up together," he said. He grabbed ahold of Calliope's hand and was looking for either Dan Paul Bailey, the front man of Audiosmith, or Corby.

Corby found him and embraced him in a bear hug. "You came out!" he said. "You're gonna love this place. Maybe it'll get you out of the apartment more often!"

Hamilton returned the embrace with a few pats on the back. "It looks great," he said, and he meant it. He already couldn't wait to bring Calliope here often; his mind was already full of daydreams about their nights out and coming down to see one of the bands that played the local circuit. "Hey, I want to introduce you to someone," Hamilton said, but Corby was being waved over by someone behind the bar.

"Yeah, give me a minute, man," Corby said, already walking away. "Opening night, you know how it is. I'll catch up with you in a few." His voice was nearly drowned out by the crowd.

"This place looks really cool," Calliope said, her mouth inches from Hamilton's ear so that he could hear her.

He was about to respond when the lights went down and the sound of crunching guitars began pulsing from the sound system. Hamilton took Calliope by the hand and together they weaved through the crowd to get close to the stage and the band.

Dan Paul Bailey came out to raucous applause and Hamilton couldn't help but beam for his friend. Hamilton, Corby and Dan Paul had been friends for nearly twenty years and after college they all stuck around the Deep Ellum scene. This was Hamilton's element, and he knew that he had Calliope to thank for getting him out of whatever existential funk he'd been in for the last six months. *This* is what he used to live for, and he realized now just how much he'd missed it.

As the band riled up the crowd and Dan Paul danced around the stage like the maniacal yet charismatic front man that he was, Hamilton was glad to have Calliope with him. She smiled and bobbed her head to the music, and she looked like she was enjoying this as much as he was.

After forty five minutes, the band took a quick break and Hamilton asked his date if she'd like a drink. She said yes so they snaked their way back through the audience toward the bar. Her grip felt warm and inviting and it sent electricity through his whole body. He felt ridiculous, like a teenager again. He didn't want it to stop.

At the bar, which was crowded with people ordering drinks during the intermission, Hamilton got the bartender's attention and ordered—a Jack and Coke for himself and a vodka soda for Calliope.

As they waited for their drinks, Hamilton's eyes landed on another woman standing at the same bar, not five feet from him. He did a double-take. He knew that Carol still lived in the city, but he hadn't seen her since she left that night—that night of the dollar store trip and seeing his book in the bargain bin. The worst night of his life. Surprisingly, he didn't feel the sting of that memory as he had expected when he inevitably saw her again.

The best revenge is to live happy, he thought. *And goddamn am I happy now.*

She saw him too, her eyes perusing the crowd until they landed on him. Hamilton mouthed a *hey*. She came over, with a man of her own in tow. He was tall, lanky, in a pair of khakis and a plaid button-up and looked like he wanted to be anywhere else than this loud concert hall.

He'd won this round, no doubt about it.

"Hi, Hamilton," she said.

"Great concert, yeah?" he said, making conversation. "Corby's got a really nice place here."

"I know, they did a great job," she said.

"Who's this?" Hamilton asked, extending his hand to Carol's date. The man took it in a loose grip that left Hamilton shivering in disdain.

As they shook hands, Carol said, "This is my fiancé, Greg. Greg, this is my ex-husband. Hamilton Raines."

"Nice to meet you," Hamilton said loudly over the din of the crowd and house music being pumped through the sound system.

He then turned to Calliope, placing his hand on the small of her back. "I'd like you to meet Calliope."

Calliope stood smiling, Hamilton knowing she understood the awkwardness of the situation, but neither Carol nor Greg paid her much mind.

Finally, Carol looked up at Grant and back to Hamilton. "I'll see you around, Hamilton. It was good to see you." She and her new fiancé walked away, drinks in hand, back to whatever section of the club they were calling home for the night.

Hamilton turned to Calliope. "I'm sorry about that. I hope it wasn't too awkward."

"She is your ex?" she asked.

"Yes," he answered. "We were married for six years. She left me last year."

"Her loss," Calliope said. The words melted him.

"Your gain," he said with a wink.

The rest of the evening went like that, the two of them flirting back and forth. At one point, during the band's second set, she began to sway her hips in front of him, rubbing her body against his.

They had a few more drinks and, with each order, he was told, "Corby's got this round." At this point in the night, Corby had comped five rounds for him, though he wasn't complaining. He was having the most fun he'd had in a long time, perhaps ever.

Though he'd been holding it in for a while, Hamilton knew that he needed to break the seal. "I'm going to run to the restroom," he said into Calliope's ear. "I'll be right back."

He snaked his way through the crowd as they got ready for the encore from Audiosmith, and he found the restrooms near the back of the warehouse. As he walked toward the men's room, Carol came out of the women's.

"Oh," she said, startled. "Hey again."

"Hey."

"I hope that wasn't too awkward for you, back at the bar. I wanted to find a better way to tell you," she said, looking down and shuffling her feet. Her hands fidgeted with the diamond ring on her finger.

"It's fine. I'm happy for you," he said.

"Listen," she said, pausing. "Are you...are you doing okay?"

"Yeah," he said. "The next book is almost done, and I've been working hard on finishing it."

She looked up at him, and he felt an almost maternal concern from her gaze.

"I'm fine, I promise. Better than ever."

"Okay," Carol relented. "Well, take care of yourself. Tell Brad I said hi."

I won't. "I will."

She walked away, back to the main hall, and he went to the restroom. As he relieved himself, all he could think was, *I won. And she knows it.*

SIX

H**amilton awoke, the** heat and pounding of a hangover in his temples. He opened his eyes painfully, the mid-morning light accosting his sensitive state. He rolled over to find...nothing.

Memories and images of the night before began trickling into his thoughts. The new bar, Club Gaga. Dan Paul and Audiosmith on the stage. Drink after drink after drink.

And Calliope.

Calliope in the curve-hugging black dress, her brown hair, smelling of honey and lavender, in his face, her hips moving to the beat, rubbing against him.

And then...and then they'd come back here, to his place. The apartment high above Elm Street. And they'd...

It all came back in flashes, synchronized with the thumping in his brain. Hamilton opened his eyes fully, and the sheets next to him were empty, politely tucked back into place, just like everything else in his bachelor pad over the last few weeks. Tucked into place. On the nightstand, however, both out of place and a welcome sight, was a glass of water, anchored atop a scrap of paper. Beside that, two Tylenol capsules, the red and blue pills reflecting in weird shapes off the glass.

He grabbed the pills and the paper. In an eloquent Palmer-method hand, the words *Thank you for last night. I'll see you again soon* were written in deep blue ink.

Frowning, he popped the pills into his mouth and chased them with a gulp from the glass. He read the note again. *Where had she gone?* Had he slept so hard that he never felt her stir from the bed, do the walk of shame out of the apartment, perhaps before the sun itself had risen from its own daily slumber?

Then, like a surprise punch to the gut that drew

all the air from his lungs, he realized that in his infatuation, he'd never gotten her phone number. That wouldn't be too much of a hindrance, however, he reasoned. He'd see her again at the coffee shop. Plus, you could find anyone within a fifty mile radius thanks to the geniuses of social media.

How many Calliope Angeloses were there in the greater Dallas metroplex? Hamilton was willing to bet the house on less than a handful.

His head still pounding, his body demanded caffeine. Not like the days that he went to the coffee shop and drank a cup of coffee or a chai latte for the sake of the ritual, but an angry demand that emanated from his bones. And nothing fancy either. A cup of black coffee and something with some carbs and salt to soak up the alcohol and clear his head of the incessant *thump thump thump.*

After a few more minutes of evading the sun, even pulling the pillow over his head and feeling the warmth of his breath trapped beneath it, Hamilton finally relented. Throwing the sheets off his body, he felt his joints ache and the words *I'm too old for this shit* found their way into his head.

Last night had been fun, no doubt. But, goodness, he wasn't in his twenties anymore, that was for damn sure.

Not wanting to take the DART all the way to the coffee shop that was quickly becoming his second home and remote office, he found a pair of jeans and a plain black t-shirt from his closet and decided that one of the bruncheries down on Elm Street would make for a great way to eat off the hangover.

As much as he thought this though, as much as it was a concrete idea in his head—*this is my plan, this is what I'm doing*—everything else in his body and his brain told him that, no, you *are* going downtown, you *are* going to the coffee house on the corner of Fourth Street, across from the First National Bank tower and you *are* going to wait for her there.

That part of him won.

With zero thought of anything else, Hamilton was on the DART fifteen minutes later, heading downtown.

She's going to be there.

Hamilton stumbled more than walked off the train as it came to its destination and he shuffled through the dozen or so others getting off at the same stop. His feet did this same, driving themselves, to Fourth Street when he saw it. The lump of clothes nested against the brick of one of the buildings. A gathering crowd drew attention to it. Someone was screaming for help, to "call 911" to whomever would take heed.

It was near the same place where Jeremy Phillips had accosted him not even twenty-four hours previous. As Hamilton approached the commotion, curious yet cautious, he recognized the young man. Not by his face, which was slouched, his chin nearly touching his chest, but by the long hair and dark clothes, the same thing the kid wore each time Hamilton had seen him.

Except now, a bib of maroon spilled from Phillips's neck and onto the black button-up shirt that he wore. It flowed down to his belt and pooled between the legs of his dark chinos which splayed out onto the concrete in front of his torso.

From here, even yards away, at the back of the gawking crowd, Hamilton could see. With the cries and the screams for help and the sirens off in the distance coming closer, the wailing sound warbling through the air, Hamilton could see.

J.A. Phillips, aspiring author, was dead, his throat slashed from ear to ear. And a knife, the chrome blade glinting in the late morning sun, rested in his white-knuckled grip, the dried blood on the blade the final vestige of his last act on earth.

SEVEN

The morning that J.A. Phillips was found dead was like a nightmare that fades as you go through your day. Except now, nearly six weeks later, Hamilton found himself back in Brad Pascal's office on the sixteenth floor with that nightmare the subject of today's meeting. From up here, Hamilton could see the people on the sidewalk below. They looked like amoebas, moving little shapeless beings. It amazed Hamilton how insignificant and anonymous every single person on the planet was, at even just a hundred feet removed.

"Hamilton, what that *fuck*?" Brad asked indignantly, though it was more a statement than an actual question. He was looking out through the window, his hands on his hips. He turned to Hamilton. "Do you want to tell me why some piss ant kid had *your* name in his suicide note?"

"I met him at that coffee shop, right down there," Hamilton said. He could see the facade of Urbana from their perch. "I went down there to check it out, to see if I could actually write from a cafe like you'd suggested. Do you remember that?"

"Of course I remember that. I'm surprised you did it," Brad said.

"He was working on a manuscript. Recognized me. He was a fan. Asked for an autograph even," Hamilton spoke softly, reminiscing on the uncertainty of that day. Because that was the first day he'd caught a glimpse of Calliope Angelos. That was the first day that began this whirlwind of writing and inspiration and feeling like he was a *human* again. And after their date at Club Gaga, swaying their hips to the music of Audiosmith, he hadn't seen her since. No Facebook, no Instagram, not even a Myspace profile left over from the infancy of social media.

"This is confidential, of course, but one of my contacts at the *Times* sent me a copy of his note. You know what it said?" Brad said.

Hamilton shrugged.

"That you *stole the love of his life*. What was he talking about?" Brad asked. As he spoke, he crossed the office and sat on the edge of his desk. Hamilton sunk into the chair. He felt like he was back in his middle school principal's office.

"I met this woman," he said. "She was a regular down there at the coffee shop. Apparently he was into her as well, and she chose me over him."

"And he killed himself over that?"

"I suppose so," Hamilton answered. Hamilton knew though that the forlorn look on his own face wasn't for J.A. Phillips's memory. It was for that gorgeous woman who would talk with him about the writers of old, of Homer and of Marcus Aurelius and of William Shakespeare and the great masters of words. How she'd come into his life and how everything went from dull to incredibly loud and full of color.

And now that color had faded. And sometimes, Hamilton would close his eyes, shut his eyelids as tight as he could, to rack his brain for the memory of her. If he could just visualize her face again, that color would come back. He could see her hair, the way it fell over her shoulders in brunette sheets. He could see the curve of her hips and the color of her lipstick, red and vibrant against her porcelain skin. All these parts that made up the whole but he couldn't quite put it all together in a seamless image, a full portrait of her.

"You know..." Brad started. Hamilton could see the cogs turning behind the man's eyes. "We can *use* this."

"What do you mean?" Hamilton asked. He'd wanted to completely forget about Jeremy Phillips, about seeing the kid's dead body slumped against the brick wall, his throat slashed ear to ear.

"I mean, the kid had a suicide note with your name in it *and* an autographed copy of one of your books. Your name will be all over the press so I want you to get out ahead of this thing. In any interviews coming up, I want you to talk about how torn up you are about this kid's passing. In every interview, really play it up. Tell them how Jeremy Phillips was a fan, and how you signed a book for him. I want you to milk it for every penny you can. And, let me tell you, you're about to be up to your nuts in interviews because I got word from New York." Brad took ahold of a stack of paper from his desk, a printed copy of the manuscript that Hamilton had emailed over at some point over the last few weeks. It came out at just over a hundred thousand words and the title page read *The Woods*.

Hamilton waited for the shoe to drop.

"It's," Brad lowered his voice. "It's fucking *brilliant*, my man."

Hamilton looked up.

"Don't look at me like that," Brad said, full-volume now. "I'm serious. I couldn't put it down. This is one of the most incredible thrillers I've ever read. I've always known you had something like this in you. I mean, look at Dan Brown. It took him four books before he really took off. It took him some time, and I've stuck with you because I knew that you'd pull out a book like this. And, goddamnit, you sure as hell have."

"Well," Hamilton said, "it took a lot of work."

"Have you already had an editor look at this?" Brad thumbed through the pages, taking in the heft of the total.

"No. I haven't even read it all the way through yet myself. It's probably riddled with mistakes and errors."

"That's the thing though, Ham. It's *not*. This book is damn-near perfect. I had Alice up front read it too and she said, and I'm not kidding, she read the entire thing in one sitting. Ten hours after work. Poor thing came into the office the next day looking like a zombie."

Brad stood from his desk and went over to a bar cart decorated with a set of rocks glasses and a glass carafe half-full of bourbon. He pulled the stopper from the carafe and poured two fingers of whiskey in two glasses and crossed the room, handing one to Hamilton.

Taking the glass, Hamilton didn't know if he quite believed what he was hearing. How could that even be? He knew that his entire countenance was different during the days that he drafted it, working from a metal table in front of a coffee house, but all writers make mistakes. Even simple things like comma errors and misspellings. "So it's good then?" was all he could muster.

"Good? I'm telling you, this thing," Brad lifted his glass and clinked it against Hamilton's. They both drank, the smooth bourbon tasting of apples and oak in Hamilton's throat as Brad finished, "is going to make you a fucking *rockstar*."

The imagery did nothing but conjure those images of Calliope again in her black dress the night of the show. The guitars wailing in the laser lights, the bass drum reverberating in his chest every time it kicked. And that woman, her hair all in his face, her body grooving against his.

Brad continued, "It has all the makings of a series, too. If we could get New York to market this as the first book of a trilogy, I think we have the next big thing on our hands."

"I appreciate the positive sentiments, Brad, but that's really up to the publisher isn't it? I mean, you said it yourself, I'm on a short leash with them."

"Well, here's the kicker. And this is why I wanted you to come in person." Brad was smiling ear to ear now and he sat on the lip of his desk, his feet crossed in front of him, colorful socks defying his black suit. "They already want this as the main push for holidays this year. They want a publication date for November twenty-sixth, right before Thanksgiving. And the advance they're offering, well..."

"Well, what?" Hamilton's heart was now beating hard in his chest as he understood what his agent was telling him.

"Well, Santa is going to be very good to you this year."

Hamilton leaned back in the chair in front of Brad's desk and looked out the window again, contemplating what this meant. *We made it.*

SECOND INTERLUDE

"Ready?" Carol said.

"Yes," Hamilton answered, his hands covering his eyes and his heart beating in his chest like a broken metronome, fast and erratic.

"Okay, open them," she said.

He removed his palms from his face and stared at the present in shock and surprise. "Wow!" he said. "I love it!"

"Now you don't have to hunch over that tiny end table to write your next book," she said, glowing.

He crossed the room and ran his hands over the

desk. Industrial style, the brushed metal surface reflected the light from the LED bulbs in the ceiling fixture.

"What do you think?" she asked.

"Babe," he said. "I *love* it." He pulled her close to him and put his hand on the small of her back. He leaned in and kissed her. "Best present ever."

"Good. I saw you eyeing that one at the shops in the West End a few months back. I told myself that when your book got picked up, I was going to get it for you," she said.

He remembered that day clearly. It was a cold winter morning and he'd found himself in the reclaimed furniture shop, surrounded by bespoke pieces that cost more than their monthly rent. He saw the desk and fell in love, daydreaming of days spent writing at it, of creating words and sentences that would become novels.

It wasn't just a daydream, it was *the* dream. And now, the desk in his bedroom, facing the window that looked down on the streets of Deep Ellum, he was living it.

They were living the dream.

He'd found an agent and they sold the book to one of the big five publishers in New York, with a hefty five-figure advance. He'd be able to quit his job and write full time.

"We made it," she said, holding him, stroking his hair.

"We sure did."

He leaned in again, kissing her, soft at first and gradually more passionate. Then, he picked her up and sat her on the metal surface, wrapping her legs around his waist.

Everything was perfect.

EIGHT

If there was any doubt at all that Brad was exaggerating in their meeting that day, the fear was quickly dispelled. After an appointment with the publisher's attorneys, contracts were signed and Hamilton Raines found his face *everywhere*. It didn't entirely feel real, even with the media and the marketing blitz.

First was the newspaper article—*Author Hamilton Raines Signs Largest Book Deal in History*. Then, the constant meetings with the marketing team from the publisher. It became uncomfortable, even with the amount of money in his bank account. He'd become the dog that caught the mail carrier's car, and now he didn't know what to do with his winnings.

While he still tried to keep up his ritual of taking the DART to the cafe on Fourth Street, trying to maintain his normal life, he found himself surrounded by more and more fans as they doubled daily, like germs splitting and multiplying. His face was plastered on billboards and bus panels. He'd never had any issue signing autographs, of being recognized, as little as it happened before. Now, however? Men and women both, clamoring for autographs and selfies. At first, he was more than obliging. This was, after all, the perks of finally *making it.* But, it came to a point where it became hard to even order his coffee or sit at a table in silence.

He also found it ironic, if not humorous, how many fans he suddenly had that had been "fans for years, ever since the first book." Given the paltry sales numbers for that first book, Hamilton was certain that many of those "first book fans" were not exactly telling the truth. It never failed to make him sort of chuckle as he signed an obviously recently-purchased copy. People have this uncanny nature to be attracted to success, to see lightning captured in a bottle. Even if it's for fifteen minutes of fame, people pay their admission for the fifteen minute show. Every once in a while, much like J.A. Phillips's copy that he'd signed when they first met, someone would apprehensively push a well-loved copy of *Great Desperations* his way as if they were embarrassed by the state of the book. Hamilton would give it a reverent flip-through. The yellowed pages, the bent corners and frayed edges, it all looked something a lot like love.

Perhaps the rest of them found copies in the bargain bin, he thought with a self-deprecating chuckle. That bargain bin now felt like a whole other lifetime, something foreign.

On this particular morning, a month away from the release of *The Woods*, Hamilton was back at the cafe, not to write or to sign autographs, but to meet with Sarah Romero, a reporter from the *Dallas Star News*. He sat inside today, not on the patio where he'd written a majority of the book. Autumn had hit the metroplex and today a heavy mist blanketed the city, not quite enough to call it rain. The tops of the skyscrapers and high rise towers of downtown were shrouded in fog and every time the door to the coffee shop opened, wind whipped in and whistled with a cold draft.

And every time it did, Hamilton's eyes would look from the Leuchtturm1917 notebook on the table and went to the door, hoping to see *her*.

Now that the novel was completed, he spent more time with the notebook than with the computer, not actively drafting anything new. He let his mind wander, let words flow from a fountain pen and spill ink onto the pages. It was a welcome reprieve from the process of drafting a novel.

After waiting for about twenty minutes—and signing an autograph, the bargain bin sticker not even removed from the book's front cover—the reporter came in. She was middle-aged and attractive, tall and lanky, with a black coat that fell to her calves and feet shoved into a pair of dangerous stilettos. Her hair, as dark as her wool overcoat, glistened with miniscule beads of water that collected there from the mist outside. She recognized him immediately and made her way over to the table at which Hamilton sat.

"Hi, Mr. Raines," she said cheerfully. "Thank you so much for meeting with me. Wish I could have done something about the weather." She chuckled and removed her coat. Taking the chair opposite him, the woman produced an audio recorder and sat it on the table in front of them. Hamilton shut his notebook.

"Thank you for the publicity," he said, and the woman laughed too hard at his feeble joke.

"Before we get started, would you mind if I order a macchiato?" she asked.

"No, not at all, of course. In fact, let them know that you're with me and they'll put it on my tab," Hamilton said.

"No, I wouldn't impose."

But Hamilton insisted and the reporter went to order her drink. His own, a chai latte he'd ordered twenty minutes ago, sat untouched and cooling on the tabletop. He took a sip from it, the sweetness doing little more than reminding him of the first time Calliope had handed him one out on the patio of the cafe.

Romero took the seat across from him, her drink in hand. She shook out some of the moisture from her hair. "Crazy weather," she opined. "It was summer until last week."

Hamilton agreed. Autumn hit quick and hard, though the last three months had been nothing but one marketing meeting after another causing each day to bleed into the next without end. The only thing now that signified a change was the weather. He knew the change had come when he looked out the window of his apartment this morning and couldn't see more than fifty yards ahead of him. The tops of the buildings just across the street were enveloped in a heavy fog.

"Well," Sarah Romero pulled a pen from her bag and a spiral notebook that flipped from the top, a classic reporter's notebook. "Let's get started, shall we?"

Hamilton nodded and noticed people staring in his periphery. It was now common knowledge in the community that *this* was his place, where you could find the famous author. It made him visit less and less, which made him perturbed.

Because if he were to see Calliope again, he knew it would be here.

"First, thank you for meeting with me and for taking the time to do this interview. I know our readers are excited for the book next month, and it's nice to see a homegrown guy 'make it.' What has this experience been like for you?"

Hamilton leaned in his chair, his hands clasped in front of him. *This experience has been hell.* "It's been great," he said. *A lie.* "It's been a completely different animal from my last few releases. My debut got a good amount of press, but nothing to this level. So, it's been good, but having to deal with some growing pains." He felt exhausted, despite his attempts to create a cheerful exterior demeanor. One thing he'd never anticipated was how much *work* was demanded of him now, with interview after interview scheduled. Meetings with Brad, the publisher and their in-house publicist had him being pulled in every different direction. He wondered, with a macabre sense, if he would be drawn and quartered from it all. Would he be pulled in every direction so hard that his limbs would be ripped from his body?

"Tell me about that, because it must be strange going from no one knowing your name to all of a sudden seeing your book and your face on busses and billboards." The reporter smiled, bright white teeth behind pink lipstick.

"I do miss the anonymity sometimes, but I have to admit, it's nice to finally break through to the mainstream." Hamilton took a sip from his chai. "Books aren't movies, they're not records. They're an almost forgotten artform in our ever-widening choices of entertainment. Even though Harlan Coben is a household name, I don't think I could pick him out from a lineup, you know?"

"Some think that you are ushering in a new era of the celebrity author."

Hamilton scoffed at the very thought.

"It's true! Publishing houses are looking for the *next* Hamilton Raines already," she persisted. "That said, tell me about writing this new novel. It's being called the 'the next great American thriller' by *The Washington Post*. Advanced readers are absolutely raving about *The Woods*."

"It's an idea I've had for some time, honestly." Even as the words came out of his mouth, he caught himself. When *did* he have the idea for *The Woods*? It had just come to him, just as Calliope had come to him. All at once. He continued, "Even before *Great Desperations*, I had the seed for the idea of this story. However, I didn't really pursue it at the time because I didn't feel like I was skilled or even mature enough to tackle this kind of story." Hamilton took a sip as the reporter smiled at him and nodded, as if she were already formulating her next question. "After I had a couple of books under my belt, I came back to it. It was rough at first, and my agent rejected the first version. So, I went back to work. Right here, actually." He gestured to the cafe as a whole. "I came here to write, to get out of my rut. I suppose there's some magic in here."

The next question came quick; Hamilton realized that she had them on rapid-fire at the ready. "Was there anything or anyone in particular that influenced your writing on this project? Any change in methods?"

Absolutely. I had a muse. Hamilton shook his head. "Really, I think it was just getting out of my comfort zone and finding a new routine. But, no, I don't think I could attribute the inspiration for this novel to any one person." The lie came out so easily, flowed off his tongue the way the scent of honey and lavender flowed from Calliope's perfume. It had been Calliope's presence that pulled him from the darkness. But she was gone now.

The reporter's smile, her lips bared from her teeth, turned "Well, it wouldn't be fair to acknowledge that *you* have been an inspiration for others. This might come as a shock to you, though I'm sure you're already very much aware, given how often you are seen at this cafe, but six months ago a young man, an aspiring author, was found dead just outside this cafe."

Hamilton swallowed. It wasn't a shock at all. He remembered it vividly.

The reporter continued, "Among his possessions was a book of yours, autographed. Did you know him?"

"I met him out on that patio," Hamilton nodded to the front door. Back when he'd met Jeremy Phillips the sun was bright and shining, early spring transitioning into a beautiful season of life for Hamilton.

"He recognized me, and I talked with him for a bit. He asked me to sign his copy of *Great Desperations*."

"Did you know a note was found on him as well?" the reporter was pivoting and Hamilton didn't like it. He'd already been questioned by investigators and the police about what happened to Phillips, and he was cleared. It was a suicide, nothing more.

"I do indeed. It's an immeasurably sad ending for a talented and driven young man," Hamilton said. "I am sad that his unfortunate death is attached to this book because he should be here with us, celebrating its publication."

"Mr. Phillips's suicide note made some rather audacious claims," she pressed. "A potential love interest gone sour, and that you had something to do with it."

"Though he was a fan, and someone that I had come to know personally, Jeremy Phillips was mentally disturbed, schizophrenic. This is all part of the public report, if you'd like to verify it yourself. His claims were a symptom of that and nothing more. Now, if we aren't going to discuss my book, then I would prefer to cut this meeting short." Hamilton was tense, his eyes darting to the door.

"What about his claims that you—allegedly, of course—were romantically involved with a woman that he was also seeing, and his jealousy led him to suicide? It's all in the letter tucked in the front cover of the book you signed for him."

Hamilton stood from the table. "I'm s-s-s-sorry, Ms. Romero, but I must be going. Thank you for your time." The stutter caught him off guard and added to his growing anger. Hamilton gathered his coat and left both the reporter and his paper cup at the table. Walking outside he was hit by a cold and wet chill that felt more like mid-February than late-October.

The last thing he wanted was to be reminded of that day that he'd seen Jeremy Phillips's body slumped against the brick of the building, blood pooling from a grin-shaped gash across his throat. The aftermath of that, the questioning by the police, the night sweats, was nothing he wanted to relive.

But, another sadness tucked away at the back of his consciousness made Hamilton unwilling to think about that day. He knew that he only hated thinking about it because it was also the last time he'd ever seen Calliope Angelos.

NINE

The club was quiet, not having quite opened for the night. Hamilton sat at the bar alone. Corby leaned against it on the other side, two beers between them, the glass bottles perspiring little beads that dripped onto the cardboard coasters beneath them. It was the first time he'd seen Corby since the grand opening of Club Gaga.

It amazed Hamilton how little Corby had changed over the last fifteen years. Despite the grey beginning to creep in his beard and sideburns, he still wore tight band t-shirts and ripped jeans. He looked like a member of the Goo Goo Dolls, not someone with a Master's Degree in business management. After college, he'd tried the suit-and-tie game with a finance firm downtown, but he gave it up just a few years into it and started opening clubs in the burgeoning Deep Ellum renaissance.

In fact, it was Corby's bars and marketing genius that helped bring live music back to the former warehouse district east of downtown Dallas.

In the quiet and emptiness, with the house lights illuminated from the rafters above them, Club Gaga resembled an old warehouse more than a music venue, the ghost of its former life showing in the high ceiling, trusses and piping exposed. The wall on the far side was still the original brick, showing signs of wear and old age. Graffiti added to the character instead of being whitewashed away. The floor was stained concrete.

Hamilton had come here after the failed interview with the *Dallas Star News* reporter. He needed a drink and a friend. Something familiar.

"It's weird to say that you'll get used to it, but maybe it'll die down eventually and you can go back to normal. You're just seeing a spike in popularity because of all the promotion." Corby took a sip from his beer. "Same thing with this place. We're packed every night right now because it's new and cool. It'll die down."

"It's just really weird seeing my name everywhere. It's never been like this. I've been able to make a living, but I've also had a sense of anonymity. I was walking from the DART station to the coffee shop earlier this afternoon and my damn face was staring back at me from the back of a bus. A six foot Hamilton Raines."

"There are worse things, Ham," Corby said. "You could be staring at yourself from the bargain bin." He grinned and Hamilton flipped him the bird.

Hamilton sipped on his beer. "You're right," he capitulated.

"Are you going on a book tour or anything? Is that still a thing? Do authors still do that?"

"Yeah," Hamilton answered. "The week after Thanksgiving, I'm on the road. Going to New York, Bangor, Boston. And, get this — the Boston stop will be an event with Chuck Hogan."

"Dude, that's awesome! Congratulations." Corby held his beer in the air and they clinked bottles.

"It feels like so much, happening too fast," Hamilton said, taking another pull from his beer.

"You know, my dad used to say, 'good things take time. But great things happen all at once.' Just enjoy it, Ham." Corby shrugged.

Hamilton knew he was right. It was a dream realized, to not just make a living but *make it* as a writer. Countless nights and days staring at a manuscript, and finally, he had broken through. All the rejections, all the heartache and that damned bargain bin were all worth it to get here.

However, something ate at the back of his brain. Perhaps it was the failed interview with the reporter who ambushed him with those questions about Jeremy Phillips. Perhaps it was just this weather, the rain now harder and pelting the metal roof above them with little *tings* with each half-frozen water bead.

Or, perhaps, it was the way Hamilton could sense Jeremy Phillips behind him all the time, catching a glimpse of a shadow that disappeared when he focused his attention on it. Like right now, Hamilton could have sworn he saw the young man in the crevices of the shadows in the corner by the sound booth, but when he turned to it, it was just nothing, a trick of light.

"You alright, Ham?" Corby asked.

Hamilton shook the thought away. It was ridiculous. Ghosts don't exist. "Yeah, I'm fine. Just taking a look at the place. It's really c-c-cool."

Corby paused for a moment. Hamilton knew he'd

heard the stutter in his voice, but his friend continued without acknowledging it. “Dan Paul’s playing again this weekend. He’s got an EP coming out. You know, we had a kickass response last time. They’re really popular on the local circuit, and I wouldn’t doubt if they get signed to a deal. Come out. And, shit, bring a date this time.”

Hamilton furrowed his brow, a deep line forming in the middle of his forehead. He picked up the bottle cap from his beer from the bar top and threw at Corby. “I had a date last time, ass.”

Corby caught the bottle cap and tossed it into the trashcan behind the bar. “Hm. I didn’t notice you with anyone.”

“Corbs. How could you not? She was a stunner!” Hamilton asserted.

“Hey,” Corby shrugged again, his signature tic, “we were busy that night. I didn’t exactly shake hands with every single person in here. Who was she?”

“Her name was Calliope.”

“Nice, man. Where did you meet her?”

Hamilton told him the story of how they’d met at the coffee shop downtown, how she’d whirled into his life and then, inexplicably, back out.

“And you haven’t seen her since?” Corby asked.

Hamilton shook his head and downed the rest of his beer. Corby pulled a fresh Shiner Bock from the trough behind the bar, cracked the yellow cap off and slid it to him. "No phone number, no messages, no social media. She's just up and vanished. That was four months ago," Hamilton said.

"That sucks, man," Corby opined. "You've been ghosted."

Hamilton drank his beer, tipping it back and finishing it off. *Ghosted.* What a strange term.

TEN

"Hello Hamilton."

Hamilton looked up from his notebook outside the cafe. Sitting at the table across from him was...*it couldn't be. He's dead!*

Jeremy Phillips wore his customary black shirt and blazer combo and leaned back in the chair, his hands with interlaced fingers behind his skull. "How are you doing? Enjoying all your new success?"

"You're dead. You're not r-r-real," Hamilton stammered. He looked around at the cafe. The two of them were the only patrons this morning. Just him and the dead man.

"Then how am I here in front of you now?" the kid asked coolly.

Hamilton couldn't answer that. He simply stared, dumbstruck, at the ghoul in front of him, looking as corporeal as ever.

"You messed up, Hamilton," the very-much alive dead man said. He pursed his lips. "You let her influence take over. Now she is coming for you. Your success comes at a price. She is coming for her pound of flesh."

Hamilton shook his head. "Are you talking about Calliope? She's gone. She left me. I finished the book without her."

"It doesn't matter, Hamilton. She's coming back to collect her dues. She's going to want her portion."

Then, Jeremy grabbed the back of his head and pulled it backward. The gash in his neck ripped open, blood spilling from the wound, pouring down his shirt with a waterfall torrent.

Hamilton gasped and stood up from his chair, backing away from the table. He tried to scream, but his open mouth produced no sound.

"She's coming for you!" the ghost cackled, still sitting in the chair. Except the words didn't come from his mouth. The gash in his neck moved like a puppeteer had taken control of it, the wound flapping with every word, his head pulled back at a supernatural angle. "She's coming for you! She's coming for you!" Blood continued to ooze out of the smile-shaped wound and it pooled on the ground at their feet.

Hamilton turned to run but he tripped on the chair that protruded from its table. He felt himself tumbling to the ground...

...and caught himself as he hit the floor next to his bed. His palms stung from hitting the ground. The pain that radiated up his arms and into his shoulders jolted him awake. The sheets were twisted around his legs and he kicked himself free of their grip. Sweat beaded on his forehead and his throat felt dry. His tongue tasted stale and gross.

Daylight poured in through the open window and Hamilton pulled himself from the ground, collapsing back onto the mattress. His back and shoulders felt tense but he allowed himself to be still. His heartbeat calmed to its regular rhythm.

On his nightstand, a still glass of water had never looked more appealing and Hamilton took a few gulps of it to wet his throat. He sat up in bed, wiping his brow with the bottom of the shirt he slept in. A line of cold moisture transferred to the fabric.

Dreams came few and far between, especially nightmares, but he hadn't had one so lifelike in a long time. That damn reporter bringing up bad memories. He had half a mind to sue her for emotional distress. *Your article gave me nightmares. Bitch.*

At his bedside table, his phone buzzed and he picked it up.

"Hello?" his voice came out hoarse and bleary.

"Hey, it's me," Brad barked. "I've been trying to get ahold of you all morning."

Hamilton pulled the phone from his face to look at the time on the screen. It was just after ten.

Brad continued. "I need you to get to the airport as soon as possible. American Airlines Flight 2269 leaving DFW for JFK at 12:20. Boarding passes and everything have already been emailed to you." His words were bullets, piercing through Hamilton's half-conscious state.

Hamilton blinked the sleep out of his eyes. "What? New York? Why?" His brain still couldn't form full sentences.

"There's been a last-minute bump on *The Tonight Show*, and you're going to be on tonight. Taping is this afternoon, so I need you to get on it. All your ticketing and hotel info is in your email. Let me know when you land."

Hamilton bolted up. "Are you serious?"

"Yes I'm serious," Brad retorted. "Get your ass up!"

Hamilton hung up with his agent and quickly prepared his overnight bag, tossing in a pair of chinos and a button-up. As for the show itself, he didn't know what to wear, so he threw together a pair of dark jeans, a white button-up and a black blazer. He took all this to the bathroom and hung the clothes on the towel rack as he showered. Not wanting to waste time, he brushed his teeth in there, spitting the mint saliva down the drain. After drying off, he momentarily contemplated a tie but decided against it. He would keep the outfit semi-casual. Checking himself in the mirror, it all looked good. Ensuring everything was secured in his bag, he included an advanced copy of the book. He'd sign it for the host.

After taking an Uber to the airport, he'd made it through the security checks and had just enough time to catch his breath before the plane boarded and he was in the air. He settled into his seat in first class, relaxing for the first time all day. Sinking into the seatback, Hamilton felt the tension in his shoulders. The nightmare and the subsequent fall from the bed had him aching in places that he was too young to have ache. He closed his eyes and felt his heart thumping in his chest. Breathing in long, slow draws, the airplane's recycled air didn't do much to help calm his nerves, but he tried anyway. After a few deep, meditative breaths, Hamilton felt his body loosen and his heart rate calm.

Once they were at cruising altitude, the flight attendants came down the aisle. A young redhead asked for his drink order and he saw a hint of *I think I know this person* in her eye.

Hamilton ordered a bourbon and Coke, hoping the booze would work to relax him before the whirlwind of an afternoon that awaited him once they landed, though he'd have much preferred a shoulder massage. While he waited for his drink, he thought about New York.

He hadn't been to the city in a long time. Not since he and Carol were together. That felt like an entirely different life now, wholly separate from what was happening now. His memories of her, of their eight years together, were like replaying something from which he was a spectator, not an active participant. As he sat next to the window overlooking the wing of the plane, the ground beneath whisking away under puffy clouds, he thought about their trip to New York City.

He'd been younger then, still working on that first

novel. They'd gone to see *42nd Street.* Times Square bustled with people and tourists. It felt so *alive.* He even contemplated moving there, especially after he'd signed his publishing deal. He had this entire fantasy in his head that they'd find a gorgeous loft overlooking the city and he'd spend his days working in the life of New York City. She could pursue a career, putting that performance arts degree to use in a city where it would be appreciated. She'd be surrounded by her people and he'd have better access to the people at the publishing house. Of course, Brad would still be in Dallas, but that wouldn't be hard to work around.

With the flight's wifi, Hamilton powered up his laptop and went over the itinerary for this overnight trip, trying to figure out the logistics. Brad had everything crammed so tight that he didn't see when he'd be able to stop to eat or piss. Directly from the airport, a car would pick him up and drive him to the studio at 30 Rockefeller. He'd shoot the interview and then be immediately whisked to a bookstore on 5th Avenue for a pop-up book signing.

The next morning, he would be up at 5am for *CBS This Morning.* He looked at the date on the top of his itinerary. He'd never even stopped to realize that today was release day.

Tuesday, November twenty-sixth.

"Wow," he said aloud to himself. He would start seeing the book in the hands of readers, out in the wild. It was no longer this ephemeral thing.

His flight back was just thirty hours later on Wednesday evening and would get him back to Dallas near midnight. That would give him enough time to sleep and get on the road Thursday morning to his sister's place in San Angelo for the family Thanksgiving. He shut the lid of the device and leaned harder into his chair, his eyelids heavy.

"Excuse me, sir?" the redheaded flight attendant startled him and Hamilton opened his eyes.

"I'm sorry, I think I was asleep there for a second," he said, pulling himself from a slump.

"No, I'm sorry, I didn't realize you were sleeping, it's just..." she trailed off and looked around the cabin. She leaned in closer, her breath minty and her eyes a light green that looked at him with curiosity. "Are you *the* Hamilton Raines?" Something about this made him feel that she'd just broken some kind of unspoken rule in the flight world.

"I'm the only one I know of," he said with a slight smile. "But, yes, I am."

"My sister is a *huge* fan. Like, huge. Would you mind if I take a selfie with you to send to her? She's going to flip out," she said excitedly.

"What's your name?" Hamilton asked as the flight attendant pulled out her phone.

"Oh my gosh, I didn't even introduce myself. I'm so rude. I'm Allison."

"Nice to meet you, Allison. I'm Hamilton," he said.

She giggled and leaned in, the phone facing them. He smiled and she snapped the picture.

"She is just going to *die*," Allison said, clutching the device and tapping at it with her thumbs. "Okay, I sent it to her. Thank you *so* much." She was beaming, like he'd just made her entire day.

"What's your sister's name?" Hamilton asked.

"Angelos," she said.

"Wh-wh-what did you say?" Hamilton asked as the color instantly drained from his face.

"Angelica," the flight attendant repeated.

Hamilton relaxed again. *Get it together*, he thought to himself.

Reaching down to his messenger bag in front of him, he scrounged around in it and eventually produced a promotional bookmark. The publishing company had sent nearly a thousand of them to his front door a few weeks ago, and he'd just been sitting on them.

From the inner pocket of his jacket, he pulled his Lamy fountain pen and scribbled his name on the back as well as an inscription to Angelica in an elegant deep blue ink. He let the ink dry and handed the flight attendant the souvenir.

Taking it from his hand she thanked him again and stuffed it in her pocket. "What are you doing in New York?" she asked.

"Actually, I'm going to be on *The Tonight Show*. So, tell your sister to tune in."

Allison beamed.

"Also, tell her that at some point during the interview, I'll wink at the camera. That's for her."

She nearly let out a squeal of excitement but contained herself. Instead, she thanked him again and went back to work. They'd be descending soon and she, along with the other flight attendants, would be coming up the aisles to collect trash.

Alone again, Hamilton leaned back and sighed. He once loved signing autographs, reveled in it even. It made him feel less like a failure. No matter how exhausted or rushed he was, he never turned down a chance to sign a book. Maybe he could blame it on mishearing the name of the flight attendant's sister, but for the first time in his professional life, Hamilton regretted giving an autograph.

ELEVEN

"My **first guest** tonight is the author of multiple novels, including the highly-anticipated *The Woods*. Please welcome *New York Times* bestselling author Hamilton Raines!"

Hamilton stood on a strip of masking tape just behind the curtain as the affable host introduced him. While waiting backstage, the stage manager whispered instructions in his ear, telling him to wave and make his entrance as over-the-top as possible.

"You're going to feel ridiculous," the young man said. He was young but bald, with a beard nearly as dark as his skin. "But exuberance translates differently on screen, so if you feel like you're overdoing it, you've probably got it just right."

Hamilton nodded his understanding, though he felt like a show animal, ready to be paraded in front of a gallery of gawkers. *Look at it as it prances around!*

The curtains pulled back and he was nearly blinded by the studio lights. He lifted his arms in a happy wave, partly to shield his eyes from the lamps that bared down on him. The cheers were raucous and loud. He felt like a member of The Beatles, with these cheering, screaming women in the crowd. Even the house band's jazz tune was nearly drowned out by the welcoming applause.

He eventually made his way to the stage, which was much smaller than it looked on television. The panel behind them, made up to look like the New York skyline, was clearly just a backlit sheet of plexiglass. A mug sat on the host's desk facing him, the show's logo prominently displayed. As he sat in the chair positioned next to the host, he picked it up, hoping to find it full of coffee, warm and steaming.

It was just water.

"Welcome to the show, Mr. Raines," the host said after the applause finally died down. "Am I correct that this is your first appearance on late night television?"

"That's correct," Hamilton said. He took a sip from the mug. The water was room temperature, tasting much like the stale water he'd found on his nightstand after his nightmare.

"That's fantastic!" The host, young and exuberant, lifted his hands to elicit a response from the audience, who returned another round of cheers in kind.

"I'm fairly new to the celebrity game," Hamilton said. He crossed one leg over the other and shifted in the seat.

"Well, it's okay. You'll get used to it. Keep writing books like this," the host pulled a hardback copy of *The Woods* from behind his desk and plopped it down, showing the cover to the camera. He continued, "and you'll have to get full-time security staff!"

A laugh from the crowd, like an exclamation point, tore through the studio.

"Any time we have authors on the show, I'm always just so interested in what you guys do. I mean, how do you come up with a story like this? Like, surely you have some kind of muse or something, right?"

Hamilton's eyes shot up. "Wh-wh-what?" The

stutter came out before he'd even processed the question. He steeled himself, took in a deep breath, and allowed his heart rate to calm. He didn't anticipate being this nervous coming on television, though he'd barely had enough time to process the fact that he'd been from Dallas to New York and was driven straight to the studio.

"What is the secret sauce for coming up with an instant bestseller like this?" the host asked, bringing Hamilton back to the moment.

"You know, I just head down to the weekend farmer's market and pick one from the idea farm," Hamilton answered.

The roaring laugh from the crowd nearly deafened him and the response to the joke made him relax a bit.

The host slapped the desk with his hand as he too laughed, though Hamilton the reaction felt disingenuous. "You just," mimicking pulling a plant from a planter box, the host held his hand out above the desk and mimed pulling it up.

"Yeah, something like that," Hamilton said.

Again, laughter.

"Okay, so the book. You wrote it, you sent it off, and all of a sudden, you're like this big rockstar. I mean, how do you handle that? The preorder sales for this book crashed your publisher's website."

"I think people are looking for good content, and in a world of constantly being barraged by the latest things on television, on the internet, sometimes people want to find something that can pull them away from all that hustle and bustle," Hamilton said.

"Hey," the host looked out at the audience. "How many of you preordered Hamilton Raines's new book?"

There was, once more, a loud response of applause and cheers, and as Hamilton looked out at the audience, his eyes went wide.

Five rows up, his face slightly obscured behind one of the cameras, Hamilton could see the young man. His dark hair falling over his brow in unruly curls. His lanky frame clothed in a black blazer and matching shirt.

Then, the young man reached up, grabbing the hair at the crown of his head and pulled back. The gash in his neck opened as blood spewed from the wound. As the audience cheered, so did Jeremy Phillips. His cackling laughter cut through the rest of the crowd.

Hamilton looked to the host and back to the audience.

Phillips was gone.

Grabbing the mug from the edge of the desk, Hamilton downed the entire thing.

"Well, Hamilton Raines, thank you for coming on the show, and we look forward to reading *The Woods*."

"Th-thank you," Hamilton said.

The host turned to the camera. "Come back after the break when we talk with the star of TV's *Dead to Me*, Christina Applegate!"

"And cut!" the director yelled.

The host stood from his desk and stretched. He leaned in to Hamilton. "The first time can give you the jitters, but you did great. The crowd loves you."

"Thank you," Hamilton said.

"My wife, she's a huge fan. Would you mind signing this?" The host held out the book on the desk.

"Oh, absolutely." Hamilton reached in his blazer and pulled out his fountain pen. Uncapping it, he held the book open to the title page and began to scrawl his name.

Except, he wrote a J and he stopped, frozen.

J.

Not J.

H.

"What's your wife's name?" Hamilton asked, hovering over the page.

"Jessica."

Hamilton used the J to write the inscription, "To Jessica, my biggest fan." He looped his name underneath and then, blowing on the ink to let it dry, handed the book to the host.

"Thank you so much," the young host said, a boyish grin on his face as he admired the inscription. "I know she'll love this. Alright, Jesse will show you out."

The stage manager appeared at his side and escorted Hamilton to the back door of the studio, where a car was waiting for him. On his way out, he looked back over his shoulder at the crowd.

Jeremy Phillips was nowhere to be seen.

TWELVE

After the taping of *The Tonight Show*, he'd been whisked away in a black town car to the large bookstore on Fifth Avenue. He put the image of Jeremy Phillips behind him, chocking up the entire ordeal to nerves. He cursed Brad for scheduling this impromptu trip, but at the same time, he couldn't be too angry. For the first time in his career, he felt like more than just a writer. With his personal chauffeur driving him from stop to stop, he felt like a celebrity. And when Hamilton walked into the bookstore, his breath caught in his chest. Near the front door was a line of people, snaking through the store. The line ended at a display table with dozens of copies of his book stacked around it. A large cardboard standup poster with his face and the cover of *The Woods* stood next to the table.

Escorted by the store's staff, he made his way to the table to cheers and the sound of photo shutters going off. He decided not to sit at the chair by the table, but instead just took in the sight as his fans cheered and waited impatiently for the book signing to begin.

"Some of these people have been here since before we opened this morning," one of the store's staff members said. He was tall, with a dark beard down to his chest and long hair tied back in a bun. His nametag read **GREG** and Hamilton assumed that this large man was his security detail in the store.

"Are you serious?" Hamilton asked, but the question was more rhetorical than anything. It was clear that some of them had been waiting for hours and the excitement was overflowing now that he was here.

"Yes sir. This book is probably the biggest release I've seen since working here," Greg said.

"Oh, come on. Surely there's been bigger books out there. What about King?"

"Mr. King gets a lot of promotion and publicity too, but he doesn't really do these events any more.

This, though, is bigger than anything I've seen him put out in a long time," Greg said matter-of-factly.

"You can't be serious."

The line of people snaking through the store, however, was more than proof and as Hamilton began signing, the line moving through with people quickly taking selfies with him and beaming as he signed with his fountain pen. His hand was beginning to cramp as he felt a blister form a callus on the inside of the top knuckle of his middle finger. He also thought the line would dwindle. Instead, it seemed to grow, this never-ending snake of people with books in hand. Some asked for a quick selfie and he obliged, smiling with each camera click.

A book landed in front of him and he heard the voice before he saw its owner. "I'm your biggest fan."

The dark, unruly hair. The black blazer and matching chinos.

Hamilton jolted back in his chair, seeing Jeremy Phillips again, but when his eyes focused, he saw that it wasn't Phillips at all. Just another young man, dressed eerily familiar.

"Are you okay, Mr. Raines?" Greg was beside him in a heartbeat, seemingly called over by the author's adverse reaction to the young man in front of him. He stared down the young man standing in front of the table.

"Yes, yes, I'm fine. I th-thought I had to sneeze," Hamilton said.

Sneeze? That's what you got?

Settling back into the chair, Hamilton took up the pen and signed the front page in his loopy signature. *To my biggest fan,* he wrote. Handing the book back to the young man in the black blazer and apologized.

"Sorry. It's been a long day," he said, though the kid took the book and walked away before Hamilton even finished the apology. He looked up at Greg, who stood next to the table, his arms crossed over his substantial chest. He shrugged and Greg repeated the gesture.

Another book thumped onto the table in front of him and he looked up at its owner to see a familiar redhead smiling at him. She'd changed out of her flight attendant uniform and now wore a pair of plain black slacks and white blouse that was cut low, revealing ivory skin adorned with light freckles.

"Fancy seeing you here," he said.

"I have a layover in the city, thought I'd come by and get a copy of the new book," Allison said. "Christmas is next month, and I figure nothing would be better than an autographed copy for my sister."

Hamilton signed the book, a grin across his face. "I should charge you double, for this and the bookmark." He blew the ink dry and closed the book. He handed it back to her with a wink.

"Would you like to grab a drink after you're done here?" she asked.

A part of him knew the responsible thing to do would be to decline, to go back to the hotel and get some rest. It had been a busy day, and he wasn't done with the promotional circuit in the city. He had a wakeup call scheduled for five in the morning, and he dreaded going on television exhausted or with a hangover.

However, he appreciated the girl's forwardness. And the hotel did have a bar…

"I'm staying at the Hilton in Midtown," he said. "I can meet you at the bar around eight this evening if you're in the area."

She took the book into her arms and cradled it. "It's a date then." She turned and left, her hair swaying behind her.

Thirty minutes later, Hamilton finished up his scheduled appearance and was taken back to his hotel in the black town car. His driver remained silent, the separator pulled up between the driver's seat and the cab. He'd eaten a few bites from the spread at the

TV show taping—cheese sandwiches and charcuterie—but his stomach was growling. He wanted real food.

The driver held the door open once they'd pulled up to the hotel and Hamilton handed the older man a Jackson. Tipping his cap, he drove off into the sea of cars streaming down the thoroughfare, leaving Hamilton with his bag in front of the hotel's substantial glass doors.

After his check-in and receiving his room keycard, Hamilton dropped his bag on the floor of the hotel room and collapsed onto the bed. His body sunk into the white linens. Closing his eyes, he relaxed for the first time all day. Though the curtains were pulled back, letting in the last vestiges of daylight in, he was too exhausted to do anything about it. He faced away from the windows and shut his eyes. As he lay there, the bed somehow felt familiar. It smelled of lavender. Lavender…and honey.

THIRTEEN

Hamilton's eyes shot open and the scent was gone. Outside the open window that looked down on the street, the sun had long set beneath the horizon. He grabbed at the alarm clock on the nightstand beside the bed, the LCD screen glaring in his face. He blinked a couple of times to adjust to the harsh light. It was 8:10. He'd closed his eyes and slept for nearly two hours.

He'd told the flight attendant that he'd meet her at the bar downstairs at 8:00. He shuffled quickly out the door, making sure he had a room key in his back pocket as the door shut behind him. Within two minutes he was out of the elevator and he hurried to the bar, ruffling his fingers through his hair, catching his reflection in a mirror mounted in the hall that led from the elevators to the foyer.

He saw her, sitting alone, her back to him. She had a martini glass in front of her, the liquid held within a light shade of pink. Her red hair was up and curled and her blouse showed almost her entire back. Even from here he could tell that the girl was dressed to thrill.

As he approached, she turned and smiled. "Hey!" she said, obviously surprised and probably, if Hamilton had to put his money on it, a little relieved that she hadn't been stood up. "I was getting ready to leave, thought you'd forgotten about me."

"I'm so sorry," he said, sliding into the seat next to her. He raised a hand to the bartender and ordered an old fashioned. "I got to the room and crashed. It was one of those times you decide to shut your eyes for five minutes and wake up two hours later."

"Oh my gosh," Allison said with a chuckle. "I've done that too many times to count. One time a few weeks ago I was almost late for a shift because I did that. I turned off my alarm instead of snoozing it."

The bartender brought his drink and Hamilton

nodded a thank you. He took a sip. It was sweet and spiced, the taste of citrus wafting on his palette. The brown liquor held a large round ice ball, with a dark red cherry floating at the top. Hamilton asked for a food menu, if there was one available. The bartender returned with a small menu, the list haughty and not full of much that would fill him up—tapas and small plates, nothing that sounded appetizing. However, there was a cheeseburger at the bottom of the list.

"I haven't eaten all day," he said. "I've had soda and water and booze, and I'm craving a cheeseburger. Do you want anything?"

"I could eat, sure," she said.

They both ordered cheeseburgers, and Hamilton was impressed. He always liked a girl who could eat. It made him think of Calliope, however. How he'd never seen her at dinner. Despite his infatuation, there were so many things about her that were left only to his imagination. He wondered what she would order before he shook the thought of her away. She was long gone at this point.

"How is New York treating you?" Allison asked, bringing him back to the present moment.

Hamilton nodded, reflecting on his day. "It's actually hard to believe that I woke up in Dallas this morning," he said. "I've flown across the country, filmed *The Tonight Show* and did a two-hour book signing, all in the same day."

Allison sipped from her drink and her eyebrows raised. "That's a hell of a day," she said.

He sighed, and sipped his drink. "It has been that, for sure. What about you? Do you come here often?"

For the next hour, they discussed her job, the joys and perils of flying everywhere from San Diego to Santiago. They ate and the drinks kept coming. They made light flirting, and then heavy flirting. Allison plucked the cherry from one of his drinks and tied the stem in a knot with her tongue. Hamilton found his hand on her knee and it eventually snaked to her thigh.

After nearly two hours of this, they left the bar and found themselves back in his room. She straddled him on the bed, the blouse and pants coming off, her legs pinned around his waist as she fumbled with his zipper.

As they fooled around, her hair in his face as she rode him, Hamilton tried to block Calliope from his mind. He desperately wanted to stay in this moment, to enjoy it. But, his mind kept going elsewhere.

One of the last things he remembered the red-headed girl saying was, "My sister is never going to believe this." And Hamilton wanted nothing more than for the girl that he'd met on the plane to be the woman he'd met at the coffee shop.

FOURTEEN

Hamilton nursed a hangover and exhaustion all the next day. He'd left the naked woman, the white sheets of the bed covering her figure, in his hotel room that morning as he hurriedly and quietly dressed. Catching his silent driver, he was escorted to the CBS Studio where he tried to soak up the alcohol in his system with the English muffins and orange juice that was made available in the studio's green room.

The CBS This Morning interview went without a hitch, unlike his interview the day before, though he knew he'd probably get a scolding from Brad for going on looking the way he did. Though no one else would probably be able to tell, Brad would, Hamilton knew. After a marketing meeting regarding the new book and going over a book tour schedule slated for December, Hamilton was back in the air, heading home to Dallas. He checked the Kobold on his wrist, never having changed it from Central Time. He would land back home somewhere around eleven, and he'd be able to be back in his own bed by midnight.

I'm too old for this shit, he thought to himself, the old phrase becoming quite common in his consciousness. It made him chuckle in the otherwise quiet darkness of the first-class cabin of American Airlines Flight 2420. *Too old.* Had he gotten to that point? Were the days of the two-day trip over for him? Leaning in the uncomfortable airplane seat, he felt like he would need at least three days to recover from this trip. On the plane's speaker above him, the pilot announced they would soon begin their landing, and Hamilton buttoned his blazer and straightened his shirt.

Back on solid ground, Hamilton left the airport in an Uber ride. As he got in the backseat of the black sedan, the driver—the app said his name was Ben—did a double-take at him in the rearview.

"Did I see you on the TV this morning?" Ben asked. He was older and his grey hair, cropped short and receding, was in stark contrast to his dark skin. When he spoke, a toothpick in the corner of his mouth wiggled almost as if it'd fall out at any moment. He'd seen that a lot as smoking had gone by the wayside in social settings. In fact, Hamilton surmised that it was, at one time, a Pall Mall that would hang out of the corner of the man's mouth. The cigarette had been replaced with a toothpick in the name of health and decency. The thought made Hamilton want to light up a pack himself, something he'd not done since college. He could envision it, relaxing on his miniature patio that overlooked the street below. Leaning against the wall, cigarette in hand, watching his worries expel from his body with every puff of nicotine.

"You most likely did, if you watch CBS," Hamilton said.

"Wow, that's great. You know, I get a few celebrities in my rides from time to time," the man said. "Just last week, I had one of the Mavericks in here. But I ain't never had a real author."

Hamilton wondered now why authors were considered celebrities? What was it about the written word, the conjunction of story and paper that turned a writer into something more?

"What kind of books do you write?" the driver asked.

"Mostly suspense, murder thrillers, stuff like that. Nothing too highbrow," Hamilton answered. He leaned into the seat's headrest, his head still throbbing. He wanted nothing more than to down a couple of Tylenol and wrap up under his comforter. He had another long trip tomorrow for the family Thanksgiving.

"Like that Stephen King guy, huh?"

"Yeah, I suppose so. Except I don't deal with the supernatural that King does."

"That's good, that's good. Yeah, I never could get into the aliens and all that crap. *Pet Sematary* gave me the heebie-jeebies, know what I'm sayin'? I prefer my monsters to be real. It's more believable that way." Ben occasionally glanced through the rearview mirror and finally asked, "You feelin' alright, son?"

"Yes, thank you. I'm fine. I'm just exhausted. Been to New York and back since yesterday morning." *And had the best sex of my life that kept me up too late.* The thought shook him awake. Hamilton blinked his eyes and sat up.

"Sounds like you are livin' the good life." The wheels of the car squealed as Ben the driver pulled up to the front of Hamilton's loft apartment.

"You know, all things considered, it could be worse." Hamilton stepped out of the car and handed the man a ten dollar bill from his wallet. Ben thanked him with a grateful smile and drove off as Hamilton dragged himself up the stairs inside the entry to the apartment above the first floor.

He stepped into his entry way, the keys clanging into the doorknob as he opened the door. Something immediately felt off.

He flipped the switch next to the door that illuminated the living room and gasped. The place was a mess. Trash and empty takeout containers littered the coffee table and kitchen bar. The place smelled rotten, like a dumpster that was two days past needing emptied.

"What the *fuck*..." Hamilton said aloud. His bag fell from his grip and landed with a thud against the hardwood floor. He took the sight in and was disgusted. He knew for a fact that he hadn't left it like this. Yesterday morning as he left for the airport, the place was spotless, just as it had been for the past eight months.

Finally, it dawned on him that this was a practical joke. He'd seen this kind of thing before, back in college. Corby and Dan Paul had come up here while he was gone and littered the joint with trash, just like they'd done to his dorm when they were living on campus. He was going to call them both and give them a bitching-out conference call.

"Those assholes," he said aloud to himself as he shook his head.

Deciding to take his stuff into the bedroom before he began to clean up the mess, Hamilton picked up the bag from in front of the door and took it to the bedroom, only to drop it again.

She was there.

Sitting in the black leather chair that was usually tucked under his writing table, she sat with her ankles crossed, wearing the same black dress she wore the night that he'd taken her to Corby's new bar. Her long brown hair fell in wavy sheets around her face, her dark caramel eyes looking up at him with a crooked smile.

"Welcome home, Hamilton," Calliope purred.

FIFTEEN

"**What the** f-f-fuck are you doing here?" Hamilton stammered. "What is going on? How did you g-get in here?" He realized his voice was stammering, the words coming out in more syllables than necessary.

"Well, I thought I'd get a much warmer welcome." She smiled again, a disturbing grin that filled Hamilton with shivers. "I thought you'd be happy to see me, but you're not happy at all, you ungrateful son of a bitch."

Hamilton went to speak, to scream, to tell this woman to get out of this apartment and ask *how in the hell did you get in here?* but he was frozen in the doorway, his knees starting to buckle.

Perhaps he wasn't home at all; perhaps he was still on the plane, flying back to Texas.

Yes, that's it. You're asleep in your first-class seat on American Airlines Flight 2420, forty thousand feet in the air, flying over who-the-fuck-knows-where. Wake up, Hamilton. Wake up.

But, no. He was very much awake and this woman, whom he'd not seen since May, was right here in his apartment.

Where the hell did all this trash come from?

He looked around the room. Piles of dirty laundry, mounds of socks and underwear at the foot of his bed, that should have been washed a long time ago filled the air of the room with a musty odor that made him gag. It smelled like it had been there for months, gathering mildew and mold.

"What is going on?" he repeated finally. "How are you in here?"

Calliope stood from the chair at his writing desk, smoothing the black dress that fell mid-thigh. She crossed the room to him as if to embrace him, and he stepped back toward the open door. "I'm where I need to be, when you need me to be there. And," she looked at the room, "you need me to be here."

"No," Hamilton stood straight now, his knees no longer weak. "This is my damn apartment, and I know for a fact it did not look like this when I left."

"Maybe you're right, maybe you're not," she said, shrugging her shoulders.

"What are you doing here?" he repeated, angrily.

"I came to check on you, see how you're enjoying your new-found celebrity status," she smirked. "Seems like you're quite enjoying the spotlight I've provided for you." The woman continued to cross the room, slowly making her way to him and he likewise continued to step back.

"Oh, settle down, I'm not going to bite," she said. "I haven't seen you in so long, I want to get a good look at you." She looked at the watch on his wrist, the silver bracelet hanging loosely. "Spoil yourself with your riches?"

"I've had this," he said, pulling his sleeve over his wrist. "Was a gift."

"I've seen you everywhere. On TV, in the newspapers. You're a *star*," she purred.

"I finally caught a break," he said, not moving from the doorway.

"Oh, is that what you think it is?" she scoffed, leaning against the footboard of his bed and kicking away a pile of clothes. "A break? When I found you,

you were beaten, like a sad puppy left on the side of the road. But I saw it inside you, that raw potential. You just needed a little...*inspiration*."

"I don't know what the fuck you're talking about, and I want you to leave," he said. His voice was stern, unemotional. For months, he'd thought of her, wanted nothing more than to see her again. That intoxicating smile, the way her hair framed her face. He'd daydreamed and fantasized about seeing her again so often that now that she was in front of him once again, he didn't know how to react.

Despite the surrealness of it all, the feeling that he was dreaming still ate at the back of his head. But he knew, no matter how much Hamilton tried to convince himself otherwise, that he was very much awake, and Calliope was very much standing in his bedroom.

His dirty bedroom, and his dirty apartment. This was ridiculous. As ridiculous as...he stopped, his brain snapping to attention. As ridiculous as it was when he'd awoken to find it cleaned and tidied that morning after he'd first seen her at the coffee shop.

"Please," Hamilton said, "I have had a very long two days and I would like to go to bed. I'd be more than happy to talk to you tomorrow, whatever it is that you want. If you need money, I can get it in the morning."

She cocked her head back and laughed at the ceiling. "Money?" she said incredulously. "Is that what you think I want? I don't want *money*, Hamilton Raines. I want something much more than *money*."

"Fine," he implored, "but can we talk about it in the morning?"

Calliope crossed the two meters, standing directly in front of him. Hamilton took another reflexive step back, crossing into the hallway.

"Don't be so jumpy," the woman said. "I can still smell her on you."

"What are you talking about?"

"The stewardess you fucked last night," Calliope said, her voice full of snark.

"Wha—"

"Oh don't *what* me, Hamilton. You know who I'm talking about."

"Whatever. I just want you to leave."

Hamilton stood away from the door to allow her to pass by him. She walked into the short hallway that led to the entry and Hamilton marched behind her.

At the door, she turned to him as he held it open.

"This conversation isn't over," she said curtly.

"Fine, whatever, just *go*," Hamilton said.

With a huff, the woman stepped out to the dimly

lit stairwell and Hamilton slammed the door behind her. He checked both locks, the knob and the deadbolt. Perhaps that's how she'd gotten in, he supposed. In his rush to get to the airport, he must have left the door unlocked.

He left the door unlocked, and she'd come in and made a mess of the place.

All things considered, he felt lucky that it was just her and not something worse. Though, looking around at the pigsty left in his apartment, he couldn't think of anything much worse than this. Knowing it would take more energy to clean it all than he had at the present moment, Hamilton went back to his bedroom, stripping down to his boxer shorts. His jeans and blazer fell in a heap with the rest of the dirty clothes on the ground. He belly-flopped on his mattress and pulled the comforter up around his shoulders. His heartbeat pounded in his chest, but Hamilton felt it slow, the rhythm normalizing. His eyelids were too heavy to open if he wanted.

SIXTEEN

Hamilton's eyes shot open and he nearly screamed. Bolting up in his bed, the memory of the night before came flooding into his brain as his eyes darted around the room.

"What the *fuck*?" he said aloud.

The bedroom looked…

Spotless.

The piles of dirty clothes were gone, save for the jeans and blazer that he'd deposited on the ground before getting in bed. His writing desk, last night littered with envelopes, receipts and scraps of paper, was cleared of everything except for the books that resided in a neat row near the back corner.

He got out of bed and opened his bedroom door, peeking into the living room. Hamilton sighed in relief. There was no trash, no stench of weeks' worth of garbage and half-empty takeout boxes. It looked just as he'd left it two days ago.

It was a dream.

The thought lifted his anxiety and he leaned against the doorway. He chuckled to himself, at first softly and then a full on belly laugh that echoed through the hallway. Of course he'd dreamed of Calliope. It made perfect sense after a full night's sleep in his own bed. Before the flight attendant, she was the last woman he'd been with, and the memories of that night were still fresh in his mind.

He crossed his bedroom and flopped onto the bed again, all his worry and anxiety melting away. Last night he'd had a terrible headache, the consequences of too much alcohol and too little food and sleep over the course of forty-eight hours. This morning, however, he was completely rested, his body relaxed.

Especially now that the awful events of last night were just part of an elaborate, if frighteningly realistic, dream.

Deciding to get out of bed, Hamilton grabbed a pair of khakis and a button-up from his closet and took them to the bathroom. He started the shower to let the water warm and stepped in after a few minutes. He let the hot water run over his shoulders and down his back. It stung his body at first, turning his skin red, though he quickly acclimated. Pressing his palms against the wall, he dropped his head and let the water run through his hair.

Once finished, he dried off and dressed. Outside his apartment, the sounds of a bustling morning made for a welcome soundtrack, though he groaned when he got to the kitchen and found that the bag of coffee grounds was empty. He'd been buying coffee downtown nearly every morning for so long, he'd not kept much at home.

He looked at the clock on the microwave. He'd need to get on the road in an hour in order to make it to his sister's for Thanksgiving, so he found his car keys—hanging on the hook by the front door, where they should be—and left the apartment.

Hamilton made damn certain that the door was locked when he left.

SEVENTEEN

The phone rang through the speakers in his Camry and he pressed the button beneath his thumb on the steering wheel to answer. It was a number he didn't recognize, with a New York area code.

"This is Hamilton," he answered.

"Mr. Raines," the voice that came across was female, with that Brooklyn accent that he'd come to synonymize with gangsters in old black and white films. "This is Detective Shauna Franklin from the New York City Police Department." The *r*'s came out soft, with *department* pronounced *depahtment.*

Hamilton wondered why the New York City police department would be calling him, but his question was answered. "I'm calling you regarding a woman you were seen with a couple of nights ago. Her name is Allison Graham. She works as a flight attendant for American Airlines. Ring a bell?"

The bell rang for sure. "Yes, I met Ms. Graham on my flight to New York a couple of days ago. She joined me for drinks at my hotel. Is everything alright?"

"We hope so, we just hope you might be able to answer a question for us. Let me preface this with, you're not in trouble. We're just hoping you can help us out with some details. Allison Graham was seen the next day leaving the hotel that you stayed at during your trip—we've already corroborated this information with your publicist at Times Square Press."

Hamilton gulped, he hoped inaudibly.

The detective continued. "We're just doing a follow-up, because after she left the hotel, she was supposed to return to JFK for her next flight, but she never showed. No one has seen her since. We were hoping you may have some information on her potential whereabouts."

Hamilton had no idea what happened after he'd left, but his palms immediately went clammy.

"But she left the hotel?" Hamilton had left the girl in the bed, the sheets pulled around her silhouette. He'd even informed the front desk of the visitor to his room as he checked out.

"Yes, she did," the detective said. "She didn't mention anything to you that felt out of the ordinary? Did she say anything about skipping out on her job?"

"No, not at all," Hamilton said. "In fact, she seemed excited to get back to her family for the holidays. I signed a book for her, a gift for her s-s-sister."

"Did she say anything to you the morning you left?"

"I left the hotel early for a television interview, and then I had meetings with my publishing company. She was still asleep in the hotel room when I left. And then I flew out of JFK late yesterday, back here to Texas. I haven't t-t-talked to her since."

"So Ms. Graham never mentioned going anywhere else after her layover in New York?"

"N-No. She said she enjoyed her job. Nothing seemed out of the ordinary to me," Hamilton said.

"If for some reason she contacts you, would you let me know immediately?"

"Absolutely," Hamilton said. "I don't r-remember leaving my number with her, though." He didn't know why she would contact him, or why she'd not shown up at her job. Perhaps she did want one last round of adventure before skipping out on everyone. It seemed so strange, however.

"Thank you for your time. Also, just want to let you know—I'm a big fan. Love the new book," the detective said. "The characters feel so real."

"Well, thank you. N-Next time I'm in the city, I'll get you an autographed copy."

The line hung up and Hamilton felt his knee start to do a nervous bounce. The detective said that he wasn't a suspect, but his mind already knew who was.

Perhaps seeing Calliope wasn't a dream at all.

EIGHTEEN

Hamilton pulled up to the curb in front of his sister's house, parking behind a pickup truck that, judging by its excessive size and large tires, he assumed belonged to his brother-in-law John. The neighborhood's old brick streets were lined with giant pecan trees that shaded the homes in golden brown leaves. Hamilton made two trips back home every year—Thanksgiving and Christmas.

He sat in his car for a few minutes, the engine idling but the radio silent. The entire drive was spent in a back-and-forth argument with himself.

She's dead.

You know who did it.

That's impossible.

In his periphery, he saw the front door open and his mother step out onto the front porch of the cottage-style home. She waved at him and he pushed all of his anxiety away, packing it in some crevice of his brain that he'd visit later.

Turning off the car, he stepped out, cradling a bottle of Paperbark cabernet that he'd brought along. On the porch, he kissed his mother on the cheek as she embraced him.

"Brought your favorite," he said, holding the bottle out to her.

"Look at you," she said, admiring the bottle, her blue eyes bright behind her nearly seventy years of wrinkles.

Not entirely expensive, he always ensured he brought her a new bottle for every occasion. Perhaps it was the cute label with two cartoon koalas holding hands more than it was the wine itself, but his mother always requested he bring some in from the city.

"Everybody already inside?"

His mother looped her arm in his and escorted him inside.

"Look who I found," she announced once inside.

His niece and nephew, both of whom looked as if

they'd grown an entire foot since he'd seen them last Christmas, wrapped their arms around his legs, nearly bowling him over.

"Uncle Ham!" they said nearly in unison.

"Hey squirts," he said. "You kids have gotten big!"

"I'm in second grade this year!" Amelia said. She was a spitting image of her mother. He remembered the same face and exuberance running around their childhood home.

The boy, Alex, was a carbon copy of his father.

"Did you bring us anything from New York?" the small boy asked.

"I'm afraid not," he said. "Not this time at least. I didn't get a chance to go to any stores."

His sister Isabel turned the corner, holding a casserole with a towel. "You're just in time." Then, seeing the bottle of wine, "Did you bring enough for the rest of the class?"

"Sorry, Izzy. This is all I could get. I got in at midnight last night."

"Well, come to the table. Tell us all about the adventures of the celebrity."

She left to the dining room and his mother helped him take off his blazer.

"I want to hear about the whole trip," she said. "Is

that young man on *The Tonight Show* as funny in person as he is on TV?"

"Let's go eat, mom," he said. "I'll tell you all about how the sausage is made."

The dining room table, an elongated farmhouse style, was overflowing with dishes, a cityscape of stuffing and turkey, of pies and wine. Hamilton yawned, overstuffed, as he recounted his trip to New York.

"The book signing was the craziest part," he said. "More so than the interviews. I've never seen that many people in line for a signing."

"I just knew you had a big hit in you," his mother said, proudly. "I still remember you writing stories when you were a little boy. You would bring me these loose sheets of notebook paper with your own *Hardy Boys* stories. It was adorable."

Hamilton remembered those days vividly, writing stories as a small boy, coming up with his own adventures for the *Hardy Boys*.

"I do have to ask, though," she said, "if you're doing alright."

"Yes, of course. Why?" Hamilton's heartrate increased.

"It's not a big deal, but I did notice you stuttering when you were on TV," she said.

"Yeah, I saw that too," Isabel said in between bites of pumpkin pie.

"You haven't done that since the accident," his mother continued.

The accident.

There were once three siblings. Hamilton was the middle child of the family, the only boy. Isabel was the youngest. Janice was the oldest.

It happened when he was nine years old, not much older than his niece and nephew now.

He walked outside to play in the sprinkler in the backyard, and Janice was out there, face down in the mud.

An electrical wire had come loose from the air conditioner unit and fell into the water puddle made by the sprinkler.

She'd instantly died of electrocution.

"I was just really exhausted, mom," Hamilton said. "But, no, I'm fine. You don't have to worry about me." He held his mother's hand and smiled at her, though he knew she could see through the facade.

"You've just been through so much lately, with Carol and everything. I want to make sure you're taking care of yourself."

"If I'm not, I promise Brad is doing it for me. He

keeps me going," Hamilton said, hoping to reassure his mother.

"Do you have any more books planned after this one?" his sister asked. "I was just telling John how good this one is."

Her husband silently ate while the conversation happened around him, though he nodded in agreement.

"I have a few ideas, sure. But nothing concrete yet. I think I'll be able to live off this one for a while."

"Maybe you'll finally move out of that awful apartment," their mother said.

"I like my apartment. It's close to all my favorite places."

"Well, I think it's too rowdy."

"Let him be, mom," Isabel said. "There's nothing wrong with downtown living. I think it would be really cool to live somewhere like that. All that art and music."

"I mean, I am probably getting too old for that scene," Hamilton said.

"Are you seeing anyone?"

"*Mom*," Isabel interjected.

Hamilton chuckled. "N-n."

The words wouldn't come out, stuck in his throat. Just as Hamilton started to explain that, no, he wasn't seeing anyone, he looked across the table to grab another helping of sweet potatoes when he saw her.

Standing out near the street, leaning against his car, Calliope was staring. Like a cat stalking its prey, she stood silently.

"Are you okay, my love?" Hamilton's mother asked.

"Give me just a second. I'm sorry guys," he said, scooting his seat away from the table. It nearly toppled over in his haste, and he had to stabilize it before it crashed to the ground.

Walking out of the front door, he made his way across the front lawn. Calliope stood to greet him. Grabbing her by the crook of her arm—more forcefully than he'd intended—he pulled her away from view of the bay window of the dining room. He knew his family was in there gawking at him and this mystery woman by the road.

"What are you doing here? Are you following me?" he asked, struggling to keep his voice down.

"Making sure you're being a good boy and not seeing someone else," she purred.

"*What*? You can't be serious. I am with my *family*, Calliope. It's goddamn Thanksgiving."

"You should introduce me."

"Absolutely not. You're crazy, you know that?

And when I get back to Dallas, I am getting a restraining order," he said.

"Do it," she crossed her arms. "And see what happens."

"What the hell is that supposed to mean?" he asked. His anger made the heat rise in his head. It felt like it was going to pop off his shoulders.

"I can make all your dreams come true, or I can make your life hell. You get to choose which one you want from me," she said.

"Okay, this is getting ridiculous. I don't want to ever see you again, do you understand me?" Hamilton said.

A voice calling his name from the house made him jump. He turned to see his mother on the porch.

"Hamilton, are you alright? What's going on? Who are you talking to?"

"Go back inside mom, I've got to—" he turned back to Calliope.

She was gone.

Vanished.

"Hamilton?" his mother called again.

He walked back up the sidewalk and his mother put her hand on his shoulder. He had nearly a foot on her in height, and she'd gotten shorter as she aged.

"You are acting so strange, Hamilton," she said. "Come back inside and settle down for a moment. I'll get you a glass of water."

"Sorry, mom. I was," he paused, "on the phone. With Brad. Apparently there's an issue that needs our attention. I'm afraid I need to head back to Dallas."

"But you just got here," she said.

"I know, I'm sorry," he said, with not near enough apology in his tone. "I've got to go back."

"Hamilton," she blocked him from entering the house. "I want you to be honest with me. Something is going on with you. Now, what is going on?"

"N-n-nothing. I'm f-fine. I just need to g-g-go."

He gently moved past his mother, went inside to gather his coat and keys and apologized to the rest of the family for his hastiness.

Ten minutes later, he was back in his vehicle, driving home. The steering wheel slipped in his hands from the sweat that poured from them. His heart raced in palpitations and he simply wanted to get back home.

He pulled the cell phone from his breast pocket and thumbed Brad's number. He held the device to his ear, his hand shaking.

He got Brad's voicemail.

"Hey, call me back when you can," he said quickly. He tossed the phone into the cup holder in his center console and pushed the accelerator.

NINETEEN

Hamilton arrived back at his apartment and paced the floor in the open living room, contemplating what he should do. He hadn't heard back from Brad yet. He held the cell phone in his hand, paralyzed with indecision.

He'd never prepared for this part of celebrity, but he knew what was happening now.

He had a stalker.

A rapping on the front door, soft and almost indiscernible from the pounding of his heartbeat, made his attention bolt to the source. He went to the door and cracked it open, the chain still attached to the hook.

Calliope stood in the doorway, not looking near as frightening as she had during their last two encounters. Hamilton kept the chain lock in place.

Right?

"I don't know what you want, but I need you to leave," he said sternly.

"I just want to talk, Hamilton," she said.

For a brief moment, Hamilton considered slamming the door in her face. However, he also worried about angering her. What if she became violent? Right now she was a nuisance, but he hoped he could reason with her now before the situation changed.

"I don't know if tonight is a good time to talk," he said. "Why don't we meet up tomorrow morning? Maybe at the coffee shop? We can talk there."

"Look, I'm sorry I followed you today. I was angry. Jealous," she said softly. "I wasn't thinking clearly."

Her eyes were large and apologetic and Hamilton sighed. He moved back from the door and gestured for her to come in.

She shed her wool coat when she did, and she wore a pair of black leggings and sweatshirt that made her look more demure and more modest than he'd ever seen her. She looked more like a college student, her hair up in a half-assed ponytail, than the gorgeous, confident and well-read woman that he'd known.

"Hamilton," she started. "I've done something terrible." In the dim light of his entryway, he could see that she was crying.

"What's going on?" he asked. What could she have possibly done that warranted a visit at nearly eleven on Thanksgiving night?

"I just didn't want you to be with anyone else but me," she said.

"I don't understand," he said, confused. None of this made sense to me, and he was still half-sure that he was dreaming.

"That girl. The one you were with in New York," she began sobbing now, tears falling down her cheeks, and Hamilton's heart dropped in his chest.

"What did you *d-do*? How c-c-could you have *known*?" The words stuttered out of Hamilton's lips. Collecting himself, Hamilton said sternly, "I need you to tell me right now. What did you *do*?"

She started for his chest, to bury her eyes in the space between his pecs, but he grabbed her by the shoulders, keeping her at elbow's length.

"I couldn't bear the thought of you with another woman, of her enjoying you the way I have. *I* am the woman who brought you this success," she said.

"I had a detective from New York call me today," he said. "I'm so confused, Calliope. D-did you—" he started. "Did you hurt her? Alison?"

"I couldn't help myself, knowing that you wanted *her*." Calliope continued to sob.

Hamilton stepped away from her as the back of his skull banged against the wall behind him. He couldn't be here. *She* couldn't be here.

He thought of the phone call he'd received from the New York City detective. To tell them that this woman in front of him had done something to Alison.

"There's no way. I was two thousand miles away. This is insane," he said.

"Don't you understand, Hamilton?" she said, moving toward him again. He didn't want anything to do with her. He wanted her out. She continued, however. "You're mine. Just think about how it is when we're together. Why would you want that with anyone else?"

"You left!" he finally bellowed. "I haven't seen you for months! You just disappeared! What the fuck was I supposed to do?"

"I know, I'm sorry. You just...you didn't need me anymore."

"What the fuck is that supposed to mean?"

She smiled now, and her entire demeanor changed in an instant. The wicked grin that made Hamilton nauseous slashed across her face. "Don't you get it? I'm your muse. You finished your story because of me. You wrote the book of your life because of me. And when you didn't need me anymore, you tossed me aside. But now you do. And here I am. Because it's time to get back to work."

He slowly shook his head. "No," Hamilton said. "No. Get out. Get out of my apartment!"

"You're famous now because of *me*," she snarled. "And you want to chase some other woman? That's not how this works."

"Oh yeah? How does it work then?" Hamilton snapped.

"You're going to write another book."

"That's it?" he said. "You just want me to write another book? How about this instead? How about I dial up Detective Franklin with the New York City police department and tell her I've got a suspect in her missing persons case?"

His phone still in his hand, he pressed the button to wake it up.

Nothing happened. The screen remained black.

He pressed the power button on the side of the

device, and the charging symbol appeared on the screen. The battery had died.

"You think I'd do anything to get caught?" She moved closer to him as he fumbled with the phone. "That's not how I work, Hamilton. I don't leave evidence. And," she smiled again, each time looking more evil than the time before, "all the police will find is another Jeremy Phillips. Took her own life. A blade across the throat."

Hamilton couldn't process. He felt the heat in his chest rise and he turned and slammed his fist into the wall, the drywall giving way and cracking. "No, goddamnit, no!" He turned back to Calliope. He restrained himself. What he wanted to do was wrap his hands around her throat and be rid of her. "Why?"

"Because no one can come between us, Hamilton," she said. "But, yes. You're going to write another book. The story I want you to write."

"Write it your damn self," he retorted.

"Again, that's not how this works. The Muses have been invoked for millennia, from Virgil to Homer, and now to you. I have inspired the greatest stories of all time, but now it's my turn. I want *my* story told," she said.

"You just want me to write a book? That's it?"

"That's it."

"What if I refuse?" Hamilton straightened his shoulders, squaring them against the wall. "I don't have to write shit."

"You will find that my influence is hard to resist, as you already know. Look what we've done together already. Your riches, the fame. You didn't come to this by yourself and deep down, whether you will admit it or not, you know that you are better when we work together," she purred. "Besides, I don't want to see the alternative."

The cellphone in his hand suddenly erupted with life, buzzing and ringing. Hamilton looked down at it.

"You'd better get that," Calliope said.

Illuminated on the screen, a New York number scrolled across. Hamilton, keeping one eye on her as she stood in the entryway, pushed the button to answer. His eyes wide, Hamilton put the device to his ear while keeping his gaze on Calliope.

"Hello?"

"Mr. Raines?" the familiar voice from this morning came through. "It's Detective Franklin, we talked this morning."

"Yes, Detective, how are you?"

"I'm afraid I'm calling with unfortunate news. We found Ms. Graham this morning."

Hamilton gulped.

"Do you have time for a couple of questions?" the detective asked.

"I do."

Hamilton watched as Calliope opened the door behind her that led to the stairwell, back out into the world.

Listening to the detective, he also knew that his next call would be to Brad. He would call and call until the man answered.

He was in some shit.

TWENTY

"It doesn't look good, Ham," Brad said. He set the iPad from which he read the email on the desk. The article, which was sent to him from a source at the *Post*, painted Hamilton Raines as a womanizer, an egotist who used his newfound fame to attract women and this most recent episode just happened to end with a woman committing suicide.

Hamilton leaned back in the leather back arm chair across from Brad's desk and let himself sink into the cushion. The agent agreed to meet him first thing this morning at his office after Hamilton called him about the girl in New York. It turned out, Brad already knew about the situation due to a journalist who wanted to give him a head's up about his client.

Hamilton ran his hands through his hair. He had dealt with a barrage of questions from the detective, but he was so far cleared of any potential wrong-doing. Instead, the hit would come to his public persona—and to the pocketbook.

"They're going to run with this story. It's going to be in Sunday's edition. We can't have things like this," Brad continued. "Especially in the world we live in now. You want to look like the next Harvey? They're stringing guys up by the balls, Ham."

"It wasn't like that at all," Hamilton said. "I just happened to be the last person she was with before she decided to do what she did." Hamilton thought about the evening he'd spent with the flight attendant. In hindsight, knowing it was her last night of booze and sex, he wished he could go back and undo it. Go back and sleep right through the night, leaving her at the hotel bar alone until she'd bore of waiting for him and leave. Her life would go on. The next flight, the next city, and Hamilton Raines would be a memory. Perhaps she'd tell her friends the story over shots of tequila how she was once stood up in New York by *Hamilton fucking Raines.*

"Look, I know that," Brad said, pulling Hamilton out of his own thoughts. "The police know that. But what we *know* doesn't mean shit to public perception. I mean, remember that hit piece right before the book came out?"

Hamilton did. He remembered it well. He'd read it with extreme irritation, throwing the paper into the trash can at home and pouring a couple fingers of bourbon while silently cursing the journalist who wrote it. He sank into the chair a little further, feeling the leather press against him.

"You alright, Ham?" Brad asked, sensing Hamilton's uncomfortableness.

Hamilton looked away for a moment, out the window. A hundred-and-some-odd feet below, life lived away on the streets and sidewalks. Little specks of life, hustling and bustling about, in and out doors, shouldering past each other. And that coffee shop down there on the corner, its plate glass storefront casting reflections, bore several tiny humans itself. The place where he'd found the root of his current troubles. It called to him, yet he stayed far from it.

"Ham?" Brad pressed.

He looked back to his agent. They'd been through the ringer together over the years. Hamilton leaned forward in the chair, cradling his head in his hands.

He ran his fingers through his long hair, the tresses falling around his cheekbones.

"No. In fact, I think I do have a problem," he finally said.

TWENTY ONE

Hamilton opened up completely about Calliope—meeting her at the coffee shop, the altercation with Jeremy Phillips, her return after months of not seeing her. How she'd just...reappeared.

And now, she was showing up at his family home three hundred miles away and at his front door in the middle of the night. He was scared. For his life and for his career.

Except, he found himself holding back one big piece of information.

The murder.

He didn't know why.

After Hamilton finished telling him about the situation with Calliope, Brad stood up and looked out the window.

"Down at that coffee shop right there?" he asked, pointing, his finger pressing against the glass. "That's where you met this woman?"

"That one indeed," Hamilton said.

"Well, at least I got you out of the apartment," Brad said, turning back to Hamilton. "But I wish you would have told me sooner."

"I didn't think she was a threat in the beginning," Hamilton said. No, in the beginning, he was completely infatuated with the woman. He would close his eyes and try to imagine her face, her body, every part of her. He would try to conjure these images so that he wouldn't go so long without seeing her. After some time, the images became fuzzier, out of focus. Now she was back and it scared him. "I mean, I was a nobody when I first met her. It was only after the book came out and I got all this attention that she started coming after me."

Brad went back to his desk and leaned in his high back leather chair. He interlaced his fingers behind his head. "We can handle this. I've seen my fair share of crazies in my day. I'll make a few phone calls. I know a guy from Flower Mound, he's kind of a PI guy. He can keep an eye on your place."

"I'd appreciate that," Hamilton capitulated.

"In the meantime, have you changed the locks, anything like that?"

Hamilton shook his head. "No, I haven't. Not yet at least. It's on my to-do list for the day."

"Well, do that," Brad said. "And you said you and this woman went to a nightclub together?"

"Right, a buddy from college opened a new bar and concert joint in Deep Ellum. She and I went there on the night of the grand opening," Hamilton said.

"When was this?"

"Right before the book came out, sometime in October. I don't remember the exact date, but I'm sure Corby would know it. It was a Friday night, mid-October."

He still held the memory of that night fresh in his mind—what he could remember of it. Bits and pieces had become hazy, like an old television that went haywire if you moved the antenna. Parts of the night were clear as could be, and then others faded from focus, drowned in static.

"Alright. I'm going to get some surveillance footage from your friend from that night," Brad said.

"Do you think I need to get a restraining order,

anything like that?" Hamilton asked. He'd never dealt with a situation like this. He was beginning to miss being a nobody, just another guy on the street. This newfound celebrity had brought a set of headaches that he wasn't sure he wanted to continue to bear. He wanted to go back to being able to write from a coffee shop table out in the open.

Brad twisted his mouth for a moment and then said, "Let's hold off on that, Ham. The last thing we want right now is even more press. Let's see if our private dick can scrounge up anything from the surveillance footage. With some luck we can get a good shot of her so he will know what to look for around your apartment."

"Sounds good to me," Hamilton said.

"If you see a black Tahoe parked outside of your place, don't worry, that's him. I'll send him your contact info."

They both stood and shook hands and Hamilton left the building. He felt safe for the most part, especially with Brad's cooperation. But that didn't stop him from peering over his shoulder from time to time. As he walked out of the building into the crisp mid-winter cold, he pulled his wool coat tight around his body.

The coffee shop across the street looked enticing.

TWENTY TWO

H**amilton sat at** the bar at Corby's place, a rocks glass of bourbon sweating in front of him. He'd gotten a text from his friend who asked him to swing by and so he braved the cold to come down to Club Gaga.

Corby sat on the wooden stool next to him, the televisions mounted on the wall behind the bar tuned to a hockey game. He sipped from a beer. In the middle of the day, the place was like a catacomb, the empty former warehouse bare of all life that would turn it into a nightclub in just a few hours' time. The smell of old beer spilled on the floor wafted occasionally and filled Hamilton's nostrils with a sweet stench.

"How are things with the book?" Corby asked, neither man taking their eyes off the action on the screen. Highlights from the previous night's Dallas Stars hockey game played on the television. One of the forwards for the Dallas Stars raced with the puck toward the goalie but got stripped before he could take a shot.

"The book is doing well," Hamilton said. He sipped on his bourbon, feeling the fire of the high-proof alcohol all the way down his gullet. "Better than anything before, that's for damn sure."

"That's good, man. You doing any more signings or tour or anything?"

"I think the publisher has some stuff in the works later this spring, when Joe Hill's new book comes out. Some of those 'in conversation with' events," Hamilton said. This small talk was agitating as the two men sat at the empty bar.

"I got a call from some guy today. Says he's working with your agent," Corby said, sipping from the longneck in front of him. As he spoke, he picked at the label with his thumbnail, the paper rolling up in weird patterns.

"Yeah. I've got a bit of a female problem," Hamilton said. "This girl I met almost a year ago, when I was working on the draft of the book. She disappeared for a while, but showed up all of a sudden. When I got back from New York, she was actually in my apartment, waiting for me. It was really creepy. And then she showed up again a few nights ago, being kind of threatening. So, I called up Brad."

Corby sat back in his chair, letting the two front legs swing up a few inches off the ground. Any further and he'd tumble back, but he kept the chair balanced with his feet on the footrest mounted below the bar.

"Are you sure you're good, Ham?"

Hamilton could see the concern on his friend's face, like the kind of look someone gives you right before they tell you that you have a drinking problem.

"I mean, I certainly hope so. I'm not the first guy to get *Misery*'d, I'm sure. But, so far there hasn't been a bunny in the pot."

Except for the dead flight attendant.

And Jeremy Phillips.

Hamilton pushed the thoughts from his head. No, those were suicides. Very similar—eerily similar. But, nothing else.

"This woman, is she the one that you say came with you the night we opened this place?" Corby asked.

Hamilton didn't like the phrasing of the question.

It sounded accusatory. "What do you mean *say*? You saw her with me, Corby."

"It was a busy event, Ham. I saw a lot of faces come in and leave that night. I barely saw Dan Paul after their set. You left pretty early, I do remember that." Corby tipped his bottle back and finished it off. "Come here, I want to show you something."

Corby hopped down from his barstool and waved Hamilton back behind the bar. His office, really nothing much more than a desk shoved into a storage closet, was cluttered, papers and receipts piled high on the metal surface. A black laptop sat on the only available space, cutting a hole in the paper mountain. Mounted just in front of the desk, taking up nearly the entire length of the wall, a television showed a dissected picture, tiny squares, each one a different camera in the bar.

Sitting in the chair at the desk with Hamilton hovering in the doorway, Corby manipulated the large screen on the wall with a wired mouse, the array of squares giving way to a single, large image. It was Club Gaga's entrance. A line of people snaked in front of the red rope that blocked it off. The date stamped October.

"When that guy from your agency called earlier, I went ahead and pulled up the footage from that night," Corby said as he worked the trackpad. "I wanted to talk with you about it before I sent it over to him."

Corby's finger clicked a button and the image played. A few people were let in. And then there was Hamilton, clear as day, in his dark Henley shirt and jeans.

And he was alone.

TWENTY THREE

Hamilton stared at the screen. It couldn't be. He remembered the night clear as day, meeting Calliope at the DART station, walking with her down to the club, being let in. He'd introduced her to Carol. They'd danced to Dan Paul's band. They'd gone back to his place. "This doesn't make any sense, Corbs. This is from opening night?"

But Hamilton knew that answer. Of course it was. There he was, in that outfit.

"Absolutely," Corby reassured him. Corby leaned back in the chair, the thing squeaking underneath the shift in weight. "You're *sure* you're okay, man?

What's going on here?"

"I—" Hamilton started. "I don't r-r-." The stuttering came back. "I don't know," he finally was able to extract from his lips.

"If you need some help, man, you know I'm here for you. I don't want to see you like you were after Carol left," Corby said.

Hamilton leaned into the doorway. He let out a sigh, remembering those awful days. There was never an argument, no single event that signified that his marriage to Carol was over. Instead, he woke up one morning to find her gone, a letter on his desk. He read it, and re-read it, and cried and screamed. He called her cellphone, but despite his pleas, she said she wasn't coming back. She was no longer happy, and she didn't want to live with a roommate. She wanted a husband.

The following days were spent in a drunken stupor, and it was Corby who had come to intervene. The pain eventually subsided, but his writer's block didn't.

Hamilton's long hair fell in front of his glasses. He shook it back. "I'm telling you, she was here w-w-with me."

"And I'm telling you—she wasn't," Corby said.

Hamilton put his hands to his temples. None of

this made sense.

Corby pressed, "If you were just being cute or something, now is the time to say something. I get it, you creative types get in your own heads and you make shit up. But I've got some private eye wanting this footage, and I don't know what to do, Ham. If I give it to him, you look crazy. If I don't, I look suspicious."

Hamilton nodded.

"Tell me what you want me to do here, Ham." Corby leaned forward in his chair and rested his elbows on his knees. "Ham," Corby persisted. "What do you want me to do?"

Hamilton shifted his focus to his friend, the man who'd been through thick and thin with him for nearly twenty years. "Give him the tape," Hamilton finally said.

TWENTY FOUR

Hamilton awoke to the sound of a bumblebee. He opened his eyes and they adjusted to the darkness of his bedroom. It was still night, but the light from streetlamps outside added a soft glow. The buzzing continued on his bedside. Blinking himself awake, Hamilton realized that it was his phone, the ringer off but the device buzzing from an incoming call.

He reached onto the nightstand and fumbled for the device. The glare of the screen hurt his eyes and he blinked a couple of times before he could make out the name on the display.

Carol.

He pushed the button to answer and held the device to his ear. Before he could say anything, Carol's voice shot into his brain.

"Hamilton? Are you there?" She was hysterical, the words coming out in a syncopated scream. "Hamilton, oh god, Hamilton."

"Carol," he said, the grogginess in his voice, but she cut him off.

"Oh, god, Hamilton. He's...he's dead!"

Hamilton bolted upright in his bed.

She didn't even have to tell him who. He already knew. The image, conjured by own his imagination, was clear in his mind's eye. Corby, in his closet of an office, long after the bar shut down for the night, the house lights dimmed. Corby, slumped against the wall beside his desk, his legs jutted out in front of his lifeless torso, his ratty Goo Goo Dolls t-shirt and jeans soaked with blood pouring from the gash across his throat. Hamilton could see it in his mind's eye and it made his stomach turn. Made his heart drop.

She had done it again.

He already knew all this, but he asked the question anyway.

"Who?"

"It's Corby," she sobbed. And then, a wail. "He's dead!"

TWENTY FIVE

He was, indeed. Hamilton had thrown on a pair of chinos and a sweater and hurried down to the Club. Carol was there with Lindsey, Corby's girlfriend. Lindsay had called Carol after she'd tried to call Hamilton with no answer. The four-block walk from his apartment was bitterly cold and he could see the lights of the ambulance and police vehicles swirling in the distance.

He went up to the doors of Club Gaga, where he was stopped by a police officer, an older man with graying hair receding beneath his cap. The brass nameplate on his breast read FRANKS. "Sorry, sir," he said. "This is an active crime scene." As he spoke, steam billowed from his mouth and into the night air.

"Right," Hamilton said. "My ex-wife called me. She's here with the victim's girlfriend."

"Hamilton Raines?"

"Yes," Hamilton said, pulling his wallet from the back pocket of his chinos and flashing his driver's license.

"Follow me," the officer said. He led Hamilton through the doors of Club Gaga. Inside, the house lights in the warehouse ceiling were blaring, the nooks and crannies in the exposed ceiling visible. The concrete floor already showed stains of beer and spilled drinks and as the officer led Hamilton to the back, Hamilton felt that lump in his throat coalesce again.

They walked to the office area, where another officer sat at one of the bar's tables, Carol consoling Lindsey as they answered questions. The young woman's head was buried in Carol's shoulder and Hamilton could hear both women sobbing, their shaking voices echoing through the empty hall.

"Hey," he said as he approached them. Lindsey took a look at Hamilton, fresh tears welling up in her eyes She burst into a wail as she reached out to him.

He took her in his arms and she cried into the shoulder of his coat. He could feel her tears soaking the fabric.

"Oh my God, Hamilton, why," she said in truncated, sob-broken words.

"I don't know," Hamilton said.

"Why would he do this?"

Before he could answer, the police officer, a man in a long khaki coat that hung down to his knees, came over to Hamilton and extended his hand. "Detective Richard Wright," he said. "Can I ask you a couple of questions?"

Hamilton felt his hand go clammy, but he took the detective's shake as confidently as he could muster. "No problem, sir," he answered.

"According to some of the staff that were here earlier, you were one of the last people to see Mr. Davidson. Can you tell me about that? Your meeting earlier today?" The detective's tone was both inquisitive and prying.

This was, apparently, breaking news to Carol and Lindsey because they both, nearly in unison, pelted Hamilton with questions.

"What did he say?"

"What did you say?"

"Did he seem off?"

"Was there any indication..."

The detective calmed them down and then turned back to Hamilton.

"May I sit?" Hamilton asked, and the detective obliged. Hamilton pulled one of the low-backed stools at the bar-height table and fell into it. "He asked me to come by earlier today. I'm having," Hamilton stopped for a moment, gathering his thoughts. "I have a stalker problem. A woman. And Corby said he might have some video footage to help me."

The lie came out so easily.

"Uh huh," the detective said.

Carol stared at him in shocked silence. "A stalker, Hamilton?"

He nodded, slowly. He could really go for a drink right about now, and the thought cracked across his face in a slight grin. "Sorry," Hamilton said, "just thinking about Corby." He continued, "She came to my apartment a few nights ago, waiting for me inside. When I got back from New York."

Detective Wright pulled out a notebook from his breast pocket and pulled the cap off a pen with his teeth. "What's this woman's name?"

"Calliope Angelos is what she calls herself," Hamilton said.

"Have you made a police report about this?" the detective asked.

"I have not, no," Hamilton said. "My agent hired a private investigator to watch over my place and see if she comes back around, but no, the police have not been involved. He thought it best that we not involve them in order to keep this out of the tabloids."

"Uh huh," Wright said, scribbling left-handed on his notepad. "And Mr. Davidson knew about this situation?"

"Right," Hamilton said. "He thought he might have some camera footage from the grand opening to help the private investigator. She was with me that night."

"So, this is a woman with whom you have a relationship?"

"No, not really. We went out a couple of times, but it was nothing serious. But then she became threatening," Hamilton said.

"Define 'threatening,' Mr. Raines." The detective was writing this information down in his notepad, the pen scratching away at the paper.

"She would just show up, unannounced."

"That doesn't sound threatening. Did she do or say anything to make you feel like your life or the people around you were in danger?"

"If I come home and someone is in my home without my knowledge, then, yes, I feel like I'm in danger," Hamilton retorted.

"That's understandable. And you said Mr. Davidson would have CCTV footage of this woman? To give your PI?" Again, the detective continued scribbling as he spoke.

"Yes," Hamilton said.

"That's really odd," Detective Wright said, setting his notepad down on the table. He looked Hamilton in the eyes. "Because before Mr. Davidson took his own life, he wiped the recorders clean."

TWENTY SIX

A **police officer** drove Hamilton back to his apartment, and he rode in silence, staring out the window. He felt the well of emotion starting to crawl its way up his chest but he held it at bay. He would wait until he got home to break down, to cry.

Corby was his oldest friend and now he was gone.

And when Calliope came back around, he didn't think he'd be able to control himself from taking his grief and anger out on her.

She did this.

She did this, and she would pay.

The officer pulled his patrol car to the curb in

front of Hamilton's apartment and let him out. Hamilton thanked him and walked up the stairs inside the entry. Each step felt heavy, labored.

He wanted to sleep. Maybe he would wake up and all of this would be erased.

After he'd stripped and readied himself for bed, he crawled into the cool sheets.

The knocking pulled him out of the semi-conscious cusp of sleep and Hamilton jerked upright in his bed. For a second, he thought he'd imagined the sound, but it came again, from the door to his apartment.

He got up and went to the door, slightly cracking it open. A woman stood at the door, hugging her arms close to her body. Her eyes were swollen with crying.

It was Carol.

He slid the chain and opened the door. Her head shot up.

"Ham?" she said, her voice shaking.

"Carol," he said. "Are you okay?"

"Ham, can I come in?" she asked, shivering.

He pulled the door open and stepped outside, the cold air hitting him like a slab of ice to the face. He wanted to let Carol in, to bring her inside out of the weather, to let her warm up on the couch. He wanted to let her in, to pour her a drink and figure out where everything went wrong. When he'd seen her at Club Gaga those months ago, he was on top of the world; never feeling more confident. Now, though? Now it was different.

Here in the unheated stairwell, though protected from the elements of the outdoors, it was still horribly cold and Hamilton steeled his jaw from chattering in response. "I'm kind of busy at the moment," he said, his back to the door.

"I just wanted to talk to you alone," she said, her arms hugging her body to create warmth. "Things are just…" she trailed off.

Everything in his body wanted to hug her, to pull her close to him, but there was a portion of his brain that actually enjoyed this. He enjoyed seeing her shivering out here in the cold, suffering from his lack of love.

You could have had it all.

With me.

This all swirled in his brain and his thoughts, these indignations, and he didn't even process what she was saying. She had continued talking, rambling, and he finally tuned in to catch the last part of it.

"...and I'm just scared."

"Yeah," was all he could muster.

"This is what I'm talking about, Hamilton. Even when you're here, you're never here," she huffed. And then Carol looked down at her feet, a sadness overcoming her face and it melted from perturbed to morose. "You were so distant. I felt like a widow."

"That's unfair," he said. "I was working. You know this."

"I think you found more comfort in a bottle of Jim Beam than you ever did in me."

The words stung. "There were times when I was lost, and you know that. And instead of helping me, instead of supporting me, you left. You left and I didn't hear from you for nearly six months."

"I'm sorry, Hamilton. I just didn't know what else to do. When you got your book deal, we were so excited. We had done it, and we'd done it together. But then, something changed. You became more withdrawn, sunken into yourself. There was no way I could have ever competed with that. Your writing became your life and you pushed everything else away. It became your mistress."

"That's wholly unfair," he said. "I was dealing with so many stresses, from the publisher to trying to write two more books on the contract, and all I needed from you was some support, and instead you up and left. Thank God for Brad, or who knows where I'd be now."

"I didn't come here to argue with you," she said.

"Then why are you here, Carol?" he straightened his back. An entire adulthood spent hunched over a laptop screen made the slump easy to fall back into.

"I wanted to talk with you about Corby," she said.

"There's nothing to talk about. He's dead," Hamilton said tersely.

"It doesn't make any sense, Hamilton. You know this. Except, maybe you also know why he did it."

"I don't know," he said. "Like you said, it doesn't make sense, but it never does when someone takes their own life. He may have been battling something that he never shared with anyone else."

"No," she interjected. "And I have to ask why you were there. Why he wanted to show you some camera footage? The only thing I can think of is that he wanted to shake you from whatever funk or delusion you're in. But even still, why would he kill himself afterward? Don't you see, Hamilton? Nothing adds up here."

"I don't know what you're talking about," Hamilton said, his breath visible in the cold stairwell.

"Hamilton. You talked about that night, the opening of the club. We all saw you there. Me, Dan Paul,

Corby. Hamilton," she paused. "You were alone that night. There was no woman with you."

"Yes there was," Hamilton interjected. "I went with a date."

"Hamilton, I was so embarrassed for you, because when you introduced yourself to your 'date' you put your hand out like this." She mimicked wrapping her arm around an invisible waist. "I thought maybe you were already drunk, but you didn't look drunk. You looked…" again, she trailed off.

"I'm fine," was all Hamilton could muster.

"Hamilton." Carol moved to him, to embrace him, but he stepped back, nearly backing into the door. "Hamilton, please. You're not fine. That night, at the club, when I found you by the bathrooms, I was so afraid for you. I was worried that whatever pit you'd fallen in, you'd found something dangerous in it, and it had consumed you to the point of delusion. It scares me, Hamilton. And now Corby's dead and I just want answers. I want to know what's going on." As she spoke, she continued to step toward him, carefully this time, like approaching a trapped animal. Finally close enough to touch him, she wrapped her arms around his waist and put her head to his chest. He could feel her sobs against his sternum and he instinctively pulled her into him. She sobbed harder.

"Hamilton, what's going on with you?" she asked through the tears.

"I don't even know anymore."

She held on tighter, grabbing the fabric of his shirt and bunching it in her fists. "Tell me what Corby saw on the tape," she begged. "Please. Just tell me so I can know that I'm not crazy too."

Hamilton exhaled the truth, as much as he didn't want to admit it to himself. "Me," he relented. "Just me."

TWENTY SEVEN

Hamilton said goodbye to Carol and watched as she walked out of the stairwell and out of the building. He shut the door, locking it, and turned to go back to his bedroom.

"If she'd held onto you any longer, I would have become very jealous."

Calliope sat at one of the barstools in his kitchen, leaning one elbow on the counter. A tight smile curled deviously on her lips.

Every bit of logic disappeared from Hamilton's mind, replaced with absolute rage.

Hamilton lunged at her, crossing the room in a

blur, his sight going blurry. He had tunnel vision and he was on top of her in a heartbeat. His hand grasped at her throat and he lifted the woman from the chair, the thing flying across the floor in a clatter. He pressed her against the wall, her head smacking against the sheetrock. Any harder and her skull may have caved the thin material.

"You *bitch*," Hamilton seethed. "Why are you doing this? What did *he* do to deserve that?"

She tried to speak, but the words came out stressed and breathless. Hamilton loosened his grip on her throat. "I did what needed to be done, my love."

"*No*!" Hamilton said. "I saw the footage," he said. "I saw it. You weren't there with me. I was alone."

"But I *was* with you," she said. "Don't you get it? I am a Muse. Not everyone can see me." Reaching up, she grabbed his wrist and pulled it from her throat effortlessly. She twisted the arm, pain shooting up to Hamilton's shoulders. His knees buckled and he yelped. He begged her to let go.

She released her grip and Hamilton collapsed on the floor as she paced in front of him.

"What the fuck did I do to conjure you up?" he asked. "Please just leave me."

"I'm sorry, Hamilton," Calliope said, her hands

massaging her throat. The skin where he'd grabbed her was red with his handprint. "And now look at this." She craned her neck into the light. "All I have to do is show them this and you'll be taken in for assault. Imagine how *that* would look in the papers. 'Famed author arrested for assault.' Sounds great, doesn't it? I'm sure it would sell a ton of books for you."

"The police are looking for you," he said. "I can make the call right now and they'll take you away."

"Then do it," she said. That tight smile returned to her lips. She looked like a predator, ready to pounce on an unsuspecting prey. "Do you really think they'll find me here?"

Hamilton stopped pacing and stared at her.

"All they'll find is a writer buckling under the pressure of his own celebrity."

He picked up the chair and sat in it, cradling his head in his hands. He felt the tears welling up in his eyes. "He was my friend," he sobbed.

"And I'm sorry about that," she said.

She crossed the small dining area to him and put her hand on the back of his head, cupping the base of his skull. He flinched and pulled away, but she persisted. Without any resistance left in him, he let her stroke his hair.

"I am a Muse," she said. "I can do anything, except write my own story. I need you to do it."

He stared up into her eyes.

"I have the power to change perceptions. Don't you remember the apartment? The filth? I did that. I can change anything. I can will anyone to do what I want."

"What if I say no?" he said.

"Then you'll find your beloved Carol the same way you found Jeremy Phillips, with your fingerprints on the blade. But, do this for me, and I will make it all go away."

His eyes darted up again, the anger rising in his neck. "You will not touch her."

"Oh I won't? Try me," she said coolly.

Tears rolled down Hamilton's cheeks. He knew she would do it, that she would make good on her threat.

"Write my story," she pleaded. "Write it and I'll spare her."

Broken, Hamilton let his eyes fall to the floor. His sobs heaved in his chest. "Okay," he said. "I'll do it."

TWENTY EIGHT

Hamilton gathered his writing tools. He would do this one the old fashioned way, eschewing the Apple laptop for a leather-bound Leuchtturm1917 notebook and a Waterman fountain pen. He cracked open the spine of the black faux-leather covered notebook and let it lay flat on the desk's metal surface. He'd had this desk since the beginning of his writing career, an industrial piece that Carol had found for him after he'd been picked up by the big New York publisher. They thought he'd made it then, and they had shared a bottle of champagne. The terms of the deal had been incredible. Three books plus an extension, with a hefty advance for each one. He'd done it. *They* had done it. And this desk, the brushed metal surface resting atop mahogany legs, was a reminder of those golden days.

He'd had his wife on this very desk as well, her legs wrapped around his waist, her dress hiked high over her hips. In their excitement and champagne drunk, they'd ravished each other right here. It felt so long ago now. A foreign memory, a false narrative.

He dipped the nib of his pen into the Waterman inkwell and filled the converter full of black ink, shaking the excess back into the bottle. He pressed the nib to the paper and wrote the first words. This part, always, had been easy. The ink from the pen flowed without effort and his cursive handwriting filled the first page with ease.

"I don't usually write like this," he said.

Hamilton pulled his chair to the desk, the blinds coiled shut, allowing no outside distractions here. A little light flickered through the beige curtains as they were jostled by the air vent above them.

He would do this the way Ian Fleming wrote his *James Bond* books: quickly, efficiently, with nothing to distract him. After his conversation with Calliope the night before, he decided to dedicate two weeks to this. Two full weeks, no outside stimulus. He would fill two notebooks with words—*her* words—and then she would fulfill her end of the deal.

Carol would be spared.

And she would leave him.

Finally, he would be free of this nightmare.

Two notebooks, handwritten, would come in around ninety-thousand words. Ninety thousand that he could present to Brad for publication. The publisher would be happy to have a follow-up to the surprise hit he'd delivered last year. This time, however, he'd have a different weight off his shoulders upon completion.

"This is a different process for me," he said. "I usually start with an outline, so I know where the story is going."

"*I* know where it's going," she said. "Just be present. Open your mind and I will allow the story to flow into you."

For him, writing always started with the outline. The three-act structure filled in with scenes and beats that he would need to hit.

This time, however, he would trust the intuition of this muse and let the words flow as they came to him. He barely looked at them as his hand moved across the page. He felt a cramp coming on in his wrist, but he pushed through, continuing to write. He was determined to get through this chapter before stopping for a moment.

"Why have you never had this story told before?" he asked, not looking up from his page.

"I have never found a writer who had the fortitude to write it." Calliope sat in the nook of the windowsill. Any other day, Hamilton would have that window wide open, allowing the sounds of Deep Ellum to flow into his room for inspiration.

"I have a hard time believing that," he said. "Writers for thousands of years have invoked your name to write their stories."

"*Their* stories," she said. "Never mine. No one else could put aside their own ego long enough to do what you are doing now. It is commendable."

"I just want this to be done," Hamilton said.

"I have seen many, many writers buckle under the stress of their own success. How many would-be's would trade places with you right now just to have a taste of it, though?" she asked. "How many have called themselves writers only to give up after a few pages? More than you could possibly imagine. You have a gift."

"I don't care. I am doing this so that we can be done," Hamilton said, never removing his hand from the page.

"If you don't write inspired, you won't give the world my words," she said.

"I don't need inspiration. I need to work," he said tersely.

"For a true writer, those are the same thing," she countered.

The muse crossed the room and stood behind him, placing her hands on his temples. Hamilton jerked away initially from her touch but she calmed him and rubbed her fingers into his hairline. He felt the soothing electricity course through his body. His muscles relaxed. His eyelids felt heavy though his brain worked in overdrive and the pen in his hand spilled ink onto the page in cursive swirls.

TWENTY NINE

Hamilton dropped the pen and leaned back in the chair. He was exhausted, but knew there was still too much work to do.

Calliope walked back and sat at the foot of the bed.

"Perhaps it is time to take a break. Come to the bed," she said.

"Shut up," Hamilton retorted. "Just let me work now."

He pressed into the back of the chair and stretched his arms. Turning his head to each side, he cracked the joints in his neck. He checked the ink reservoir in the pen and filled it up from the inkwell.

"Hamilton," Calliope cooed from the bed. "You seem tense now. That's not conducive to good writing. Come to the bed. Let me relieve your stress."

"No." He flipped the notebook to the empty page where he'd left off and, reading what he'd written already, put the nib to the page and began again.

"You're not going to be able to work like that forever," she purred. "You're going to need me."

"I don't need you," he said, never looking up from the lined pages of the notebook. "Just tell me what you want written."

"Come to bed and I will fill your mind with all the wondrous things that are in mine."

He sat the pen down on the desk and sighed. Glancing at the watch that hung from a nylon strap on his wrist, he saw the hands making a right angle, the little hand hovering over the three. "Fine," he relented, placing the notebook's fabric bookmark in between the sheets and closing it. "But I want to sleep. When I wake up tomorrow morning, we begin again."

"Sounds like a pleasant compromise to me, my love."

"Don't call me that," Hamilton said indignantly

as he stood from the chair. "Right now, all we are is an employer and employee. I'm your ghost writer, and that's it."

"Whatever makes you happy," she said, scooting over on the mattress.

Hamilton pulled off his boots and chinos and fell into the sheets. He pulled the comforter close to his shoulders and turned to face away from Calliope.

As he fell asleep, he felt her touch on the back of his skull, feeling her fingertips trace his hairline. She whispered, the words unintelligible except for in his imagination. In his mind's eye, as he drifted off, he saw everything.

THIRTY

Hamilton woke up groggy, his body aching. Sweat had saturated the fabric of his pillowcase and it now felt cold under his temple. Chills ran through his bones.

He turned over and found himself alone in the bed. She'd gone again, though he knew she'd return. They still had work to do. He would continue on without her until she reappeared.

Except he didn't think he'd be able to work today.

He could think of only one other time his body had ached like this, and it was in college. He'd been diagnosed with the flu, and it had knocked him on his ass for nearly a week, with a cough that lingered for a month after. That's what this felt like now, the body aches and chills and the sweat pooling from his head and soaking into his sheets.

Gingerly lifting himself from his bed, Hamilton crossed his room and went to the bathroom. He turned the knobs in the shower, the process taking more effort than usual. As he waited for the water to warm up, he rested his forehead on the cool marble counter. He felt the heat radiate from his temples. He looked at himself in the mirror above the sink. His eyes were sunken and dark circles orbited them.

He stripped out of his boxer shorts and stepped into the shower. The water, steam wafting into the open air above the shower head, was warm but his body still shivered beneath the flow. Eventually he knelt onto the floor of the stall, dropping his butt to the ground, his knees pulled up to his chest. He stayed like that for nearly twenty minutes, letting the water spill all around him. It whirled into the drain beneath his feet and with his head cradled on his knees, he watched it disappear.

The water began to lose its warmth and he pulled himself up from the upright fetal position, turning the knobs to stop the flow. He opened the curtain and pulled a towel hanging from the rack outside it. He wrapped it around his shoulders, hugging himself for warmth, his teeth chattering and his muscles quivering. The mirror had fogged over from the steam trapped in the bathroom. Hamilton reached up to wipe the glass clean.

The face staring back at him was not his own.

Hamilton screamed out, but the sound was trapped in his throat that felt as if it were lined in razorblades.

Jeremy Phillips stared back at him. "Surprised to see me, Hamilton?"

His feet began to backpedal and, tripping on the rug, Hamilton fell onto the toilet seat, his body landing hard on the porcelain. Pain radiated from his tailbone. He looked up again, and the face of Jeremy Phillips peered up back at him through the mirror.

"You really thought you'd get away with it, didn't you?" the ghost in the mirror said.

Get away with what? What is going on here?

"I'm dreaming," Hamilton said, his voice rasp and whispered. "You're not real. This isn't real."

"Think about it, Hamilton," the visage of Jeremy Phillips said. "Think about what you did."

Hamilton lowered his head and shook it, his hair falling around his brow. Water, mixed with sweat and tears, fell from his face and splashed onto the tile. He began to feel nauseous. "I didn't do it."

"Yes you did, Hamilton. You did it. Admit it."

"No."

"You won't be able to hide from the truth forever."

"I didn't."

"You *did.* Say it, Hamilton. Out loud."

Hamilton held his head low, hoping that the image in his mirror would disappear—hoping that he'd wake up from this nightmare.

But the voice continued. "Don't you remember, Hamilton? Don't you remember meeting me at the cafe on Fourth Avenue that warm early spring afternoon? I was so excited to meet you, to meet my idol. Instead, you took everything from me."

Hamilton replayed the day in his mind. Leaving Brad's office, he'd crossed the street to Urbana, the coffee shop on the corner he'd never noticed before. He sat on the patio at a metal table, sipping on an iced latte when he saw the young man, not three yards away, writing furiously at a manuscript by hand, the pen scribbling away at a black notebook. It looked like a Moleskine, the elastic band flopped off to the side.

The young writer had noticed Hamilton watching him and his eyes went wide. Slowly, he got up and approached Hamilton.

"Remember our conversation, Hamilton?" the voice from the mirror implored.

His brain, with his temples thumping from an excruciating headache, his body shivering from fever, recollected the entire encounter.

"I told you that you were one of my favorites."

In his memory, he stayed in his seat as Jeremy Phillips gushed about *Great Desperations* and produced a copy for Hamilton to sign it.

"I signed your book," Hamilton said.

"But that's not all you did. You asked me about what I was writing, and I told you. The story about the boys in the woods. Their treehouse."

Hamilton remembered the black notebook. The young man had handed it over as well. And then...

No.

It couldn't be real. Hamilton shook the thought from his head.

"You stole my story, Hamilton Raines," Jeremy Phillips said.

No.

No.

No.

He'd signed the well-loved copy of *Great Desperations*, and while Phillips admired the signature and inscription, Hamilton had...

He'd switched them.

They looked exactly the same, both notebooks. The one resting atop his MacBook, and the one Phillips offered for him to flip through. The young man's cursive handwriting filling every page. Hamilton glanced through the pages, read a few paragraphs. It was enthralling. The characters spoke with a realism that jumped from the page.

And then he swapped them. With an amateur sleight-of-hand, he'd handed his own notebook back to Jeremy, taking the young man's.

"You stole my story," Jeremy Phillips repeated from the mirror.

The tears came even harder now, and Hamilton wiped them from his eyes. Snot dripped from his nostrils as he remembered his heart racing when he'd done it. Jeremy Phillips had left the cafe, never opening the notebook that Hamilton had handed back to him, never once cracking it to ensure it was his.

But why would he have any indication that it wasn't?

The kid had probably been high on excitement, having met his favorite author, and Hamilton had stolen the notebook from him.

Once he'd gotten home, he quickly got to work, transcribing all the written words. Self-editing as he went, he typed it into a Word document on his laptop. He felt guilty. But he pushed the guilt down. The kid would go on to write new things, to create again.

But Hamilton *needed* this. He needed a breakthrough.

So, he took the notebook and once he had the entire thing typed up, he took it to Brad.

"I found you, and I demanded it back," Jeremy continued.

Hamilton relived the last time he'd seen Jeremy. The young man grabbing him by the collar, pushing him against the brick of the building. Hamilton remembered being indignant, that this amateur had the audacity to put his hands on him.

"You were talking about Calliope," Hamilton said.

"Calliope isn't *real*. You know this. You made her up. To help you cope with what you'd done. You stole my story and made up a muse so that you wouldn't face the truth—that what you took didn't belong to you. It didn't come from your brain. It came from *mine*."

The insinuation made his nausea gurgle from his stomach and into his esophagus. Bile forced its way up his throat and Hamilton grabbed the trashcan next to the toilet just in time. Hot vomit spewed from his lips, splashing on old receipts and toilet paper in the can.

"No..." Hamilton began to argue before he felt the bile wretch up once more as he vomited into the trash can. "That's not true. She came to me."

"Look at me, Hamilton."

The voice from the mirror wasn't Jeremy's this time, however. No, it was a voice that he'd become quite familiar with over the last year. Hamilton couldn't bring himself to look up. There was no way this was happening.

The voice repeated. "Look at me."

Slowly, with his eyes closed, Hamilton lifted his head to the mirror. His eyes opened.

And there she was.

Calliope had replaced the man in the mirror. Her smile, what he was once enticed by, had a dangerous curve to it.

Hamilton felt the tears come, full sobs heaved in his chest. "This isn't real!" he exclaimed. Reaching for anything, he found the handle of the plunger next to the toilet. He heaved it at the mirror, the wooden staff hitting the glass. Spiderweb cracks shattered Calliope's face into newly-created sections. A hundred little Calliopes, all with that same man-eating grin.

"I didn't make you up!" he screamed.

"Maybe," she said. "Maybe that's all I am. Made up by the imaginations of writers and artists from all of history. You are just the latest in the line."

Hamilton stood from the toilet seat. His feet wobbled beneath him, his knees shaking and weak—either from the vomiting or from this hallucination, he didn't really know which. But he stood and, with unsure steps, went back into the bedroom. He went to the writing desk, shuffling around the notebooks on the surface. There were the two that he'd done the most recent work in, his handwriting sloppy yet intelligible.

A third Moleskine sat dejected on the corner of the desk, the corners frayed from being shoved into a backpack, the elastic band that looped around the front losing its hold and laying slack.

He felt the lump in his throat even before his shaking fingers took ahold of the black notebook. He could hardly get the elastic band released as his hands shivered. Finally, he was able to open it. On the inside, the first page was signed **J.A. PHILLIPS**.

Hamilton never felt his knees give out, never felt his body crumple to the floor. The lights were out before his head smacked against the carpet.

THIRTY ONE

"**The hard drives** in the DVR were formatted, which means there's no way to extract the data in this state," the technician said. His name was Stephen Goodard, a graduate of University of North Texas and a technology investigator with the Dallas police department. He'd gotten the job right out of college, putting his skills to work here instead of at a big-box geek squad factory. He pushed the rolled sleeves of his dingy white oxford button-up over his forearms and cracked his knuckles. "I can attempt a forensics data recovery, but that could take days."

Detective Richard Wright stood up from the desk and paced the floor. "That would take too long. We need to act quickly on this and get the arrest warrant." He'd spoken to the investigator in New York in charge of the case of the deceased flight attendant. They'd spent hours matching up evidence. It all clicked into place.

"What about security camera footage from buildings near the place? Surely one or two of them have cameras facing the street or sidewalks," Goddard suggested. "I can pull the data from the hard drives if they exist."

The investigator nodded. "Yeah, if we can get something that even looks like Raines walking to or away from the club, that should be enough to stick him with it."

Goddard turned back to the terminal display at his computer desk. Over his shoulder he said, "I'll get on it."

"Good," Wright said. "I'm going to call his agent. We're going to need friends for this one."

THIRTY TWO

Brad Pascal was at home when he got the call. He'd poured two fingers of Woodford Reserve over a couple of ice cubes and was reading over the police report. The three suicides were too much alike, too coincidental to be suicides, despite the time and distance separating them.

The one piece of evidence that couldn't be dismissed, no matter how much his brain told him to do so, stuck out to him. It was on all three blades, even the one found in the dead grip of the girl up in New York. All three the same brand.

That's why he needed the bourbon.

The phone rang again and he finally picked it up.

He swiped the screen and held the device to his ear as he sat at the metal patio table outside.

Beth had gone to bed about an hour ago and he liked to spend his waning waking hours out here at night, relaxing with his two fingers of booze before hitting the sack himself.

"Did you get it?" Before Brad had even been able to get the "Hello?" out of his mouth, the voice on the other end asked the question.

Brad took a sip from the rocks glass, the taste of smoked oak and apples lingering on his palette. "I did," he said, swallowing, feeling the fire down his throat.

"Can you get him to come in?"

"Yeah, I think I can."

"We want this quiet," the voice said.

"Yeah no shit. So do I," Brad said. "It's not just your name on this thing, or his. It's mine too. Do you know what these kinds of allegations are going to do to my agency?"

"The same thing they are going to do to our brand if we don't get this under control."

Brad took further instruction from the president of the publishing company and hung up, his heart still racing from the implications of what he was now dealing with. He knew that his golden goose was too good to be true, despite riding the tail to the very end. He should have seen this coming, though. Though he wouldn't admit it to anyone else, he blamed himself.

Brad thought back to that meeting last winter, how broken and withdrawn Hamilton had looked at the time. It was his idea that his client go out, find a new routine. He'd suggested a coffee shop, just something to get the writer out of the apartment and back into normal life. Find something that would jumpstart the process so that they wouldn't get dropped by the publisher. But like an unwinding cable car, his client snapped.

He would have never thought it would come to *this*.

THIRTY THREE

Hamilton awoke once again, and his body felt like he'd been hit by a carload of assholes. He felt his muscles contracting and shivering from the fever. He blinked, the fuzz of the beige carpet that lined his bedroom floor blurred against his vision as the world came back into focus.

He was on the floor, he gathered that much.

Conversations came back to him.

And then the notebook. The notebook on his desk.

No. He couldn't bring himself to face the allegations that the man in the mirror brought down on him. But, with an exhale, he knew it was the truth.

Hamilton, his body prone on the carpet, thought back to that day that Jeremy Phillips came up on him, a block from the coffee shop. The young man's eyes were wild, accusing. He looked like he'd lost sleep over the culmination of that moment that he'd shoved Hamilton against the exterior brick of the building.

"You stole it!" he'd said. "You stole my book!"

Hamilton had heard something entirely different. Or, his brain had translated the words into something that made sense to him at the moment. He'd taken the book, of course, but then he'd buried the act below his own consciousness.

Remembering that one altercation brought back every other act that he'd shoved to the back of his brain. It all flooded him with a sorrow and sickness that he could not bear. Hamilton laid sprawled on his bedroom floor and began crying. Crying for Corby, and for Allison.

And for Jeremy, whose only sin was showing the novel he'd written to his hero.

Each one of them met a violent and bloody end, their necks slashed with a razor blade, the kind of blade so sharp that you wouldn't even know that you'd been cut until your t-shirt was soaked with your own blood and your airway was choked full of it.

Hamilton cried, his tears falling into the carpet and creating twin pools on either side of his head as they streamed down his face. Pulling himself up into a sitting position, he saw them both. They sat at the edge of his bed, their feet dangling above the footboard.

The woman, that he now knew he had made up, that he'd conjured and created to cope with his own shame and disgrace. With her, the ghost of the young man from whom he'd taken the story. He'd committed the biggest sin of all.

Hamilton stole the story.

They looked down at him, both with murderous grins on their faces.

"Get up, Hamilton," Calliope said.

"No," he responded. "I made you up. You're not real."

"Whether you think that or not doesn't matter," she said. "Listen to that noise outside."

Hamilton stilled himself and listened. Sirens. The rising and falling high-pitch of police sirens wailed in the distance. Every second, the sound grew louder and Hamilton imagined the drivers of the police cruisers speeding to his apartment.

"There's only one way out," Jeremy said.

Hamilton looked up at him, the young writer's face towering over him as he sat on the floor. He felt like a child, looking up at his two disappointed parents after he'd pissed the bed.

Jeremy looked down at him and held out his hand. "There's only one way out," he repeated.

Hamilton realized that the young man's hand was held out. And in it, a knife. The curved metal handle housed the razorblade that could be retracted or drawn with a flick of a lever on the side. Hamilton took it apprehensively.

It felt familiar, the way the handle conformed to his grip. As he looked it over in his hand, he knew what he needed to do.

He'd done it before.

It started when he was seven years old.

When he dropped the live electrical line in the water puddle that hot summer day, he didn't know exactly what would happen, but he'd learned in school that electricity and water together made a deadly combination.

He wanted to see what would happen, and after it did, he tucked the memory away in some crevice of his psyche. It was a secret he'd kept even from himself.

"It's the only escape now, Hamilton," Calliope

said. Jeremy nodded in agreement, the slit in his throat opening slightly as he did.

Hamilton's hand, shaking from either nervousness or sickness, reached out, his pallid fingers clasping the tool.

Flashes of memories came back, first of Jeremy Phillips. The young man walking down the sidewalk on a Sunday morning, walking toward Urbana. Hamilton had waited for him, hidden behind the corner where the building met the alleyway. Any number of people could have seen him, could have spoiled the act, but evil fortune had smiled down on him. As Jeremy walked by the alleyway's opening, Hamilton snuck out, the blade extracted from its sheath and, coming up behind the young man, pulled him back toward the mouth of the dark alley while simultaneously slashing the blade against the unsuspecting amateur writer's throat, blood immediately pouring from the wound.

Jeremy had grasped for his neck as Hamilton led him to the ground, losing pints of blood in just a few seconds.

He left him there, placing the blade in the young man's hand. No one could know what he'd done, either with the notebook or with Jeremy. Like Janice's death, it was a secret he'd meant to keep from everyone, including himself.

The same acts were similar with both the flight attendant and with Corby, the blades doing their work quickly. Hamilton had left all three of them with their own blade, making it look like they'd done it to themselves.

And he thought of Janice, dead at eight years old, face down in the mud.

All these images, these memories, flooded back to his brain now as he stared at the razor in his hand.

Once more, he looked up at the apparitions on his bedside, hoping for some other avenue to escape this fate. There was none, though. No other way out. It had to be this way.

Hamilton stood, his legs feeling weak beneath his body, and looked out the window down to the streets of Deep Ellum below. Police cruisers pulled up to the building, their lights rotating, their sirens blaring. This was it.

Hamilton took one last look at the writing desk, the final vestiges of his life.

The blade did its job.

EPILOGUE

Brad stood at the apartment door and rapped at it with his knuckles. His tie, looped through the collar of his haphazardly-buttoned shirt, was loose and hanging low. His pits were stained with sweat already, despite the cold outside. It was a nervous sweat and it beaded in his hairline as well.

"Ham, buddy?" he called out.

No answer.

He held his ear to the door and listened inside for any movement, a rustling of feet on the carpet. Again, nothing.

He knocked and again called out, this time a little

louder, "Hamilton? Hey, it's Brad. Come open the door."

"Stand aside, Mr. Pascal," the police officer who accompanied him said. After talking with Detective Wright, Brad agreed to come to Hamilton himself, to assuage his client to allow himself to be taken into custody.

He moved away from the door and the officer shouldered the door once, twice, and once more until the lock gave way, the door frame cracking beneath the stocky man's force.

With a kick, the door swung open and the smell of decay hit Brad in the face with a nauseating force. He nearly gagged on it and pulled the elbow of his blazer to his nose.

Inside, it was dark and unlit, except for the light seeping through the open doorway but Brad could see the mess in the apartment. He stepped inside slowly. "Hamilton? We're coming in."

Once inside, Brad flipped the switch on the wall in the kitchen. Keeping his nose covered, he could see the take-out boxes, the styrofoam containers, all stacked haphazardly on the counter top. The trashcan overflowed with papers and bills. Beer bottles were strewn everywhere. He couldn't believe Hamilton lived like this, but in the back of his mind, he knew it was to be expected.

Hamilton's depression had been bubbling under the surface. This was the manifestation of it, this disgusting mess.

As Brad called out, still to no answer, he crossed the apartment to the bedroom, the one that looked out over the street and to Deep Ellum below. He pushed the door open lightly and saw him there. Letting out a gasp, he was on top of Hamilton in two steps, kneeling next to him.

The man's body was cold. Brad quickly realized the carpet was soaked in blood around him. His knees sank into the sticky wetness. "Ham," he said, "wake up buddy. Come on, Ham."

But he knew the man was gone, his body full of dead weight. Taking in the room, he saw the pages of a manuscript everywhere. He picked up a piece of paper from the ground, the bottom half red and saturated with Hamilton's blood. He recognized the words from the book they'd published last year, though they were written in a hand that he didn't recognize. The words, though, were definitely from that book. The one that turned Hamilton into an overnight rockstar.

At the top of the page, before several handwritten paragraphs, it read *The Woods - First Draft - Jeremy*

Phillips.

Who the hell is Jeremy Phillips? The name rang a bell in his mind. Brad had heard it somewhere before, but couldn't quite put his finger on it.

Behind him, the police officer radioed in for backup and for an ambulance, but it was no use. Hamilton was gone.

Brad got up from his knees, feeling the wet fabric sticking to his legs. He looked around the room, taking it all in. On the writing table in the corner, a notebook splayed open. Brad went to it. Next to the notebook, a scrap of paper held a note written in feminine cursive.

Thank you for last night. I'll see you again soon, the note read.

He looked back to make sure the officer had left the room, and picked up the open notebook on the table, flipping through the pages.

Hamilton had written an entire novel in this thing.

Through the stench of everything else, though, Brad caught a hint of perfume on the pages. A rustling in the living room hinted that the officer who had accompanied him was on his way back into the bedroom. Brad took one more glance toward the door.

Before putting the notebook, and the one beneath

it, in the breast pocket of his peacoat, the covers clasped closed with their elastic band, he held the pages to his nose and inhaled. He swore he could smell lavender.

Lavender and honey.

THE END

SPECIAL ACKNOWLEDGEMENTS

This book was written in the middle of the COVID-19 pandemic. I was working on a novel called *American Atonement* but found myself drawn to this story, so I did something I've never done before—I sat a book aside and began this one. It came out fast and whole and even more sinister than I had originally envisioned.

Like all of my books, I have several people to thank for their help in bringing it to life. First and foremost, my wife Jennifer and her unwavering support in this endeavor. It's many early mornings and late nights of me clacking away at a keyboard or scribbling in a journal. It's hours-long drives to book signing events and she takes it all in stride. I love you.

My editor, Brandon Biggers, is paramount to these things taking shape and making sense. All the hours spent reading and going over scenes and arcs to ensure it all connects. Without his guiding hand, these stories would be an absolute mess.

Charles D'Amico, thank you for believing in my works and writing and for bringing me onboard with Blue Handle Publishing.

For everyone else, thank you:

Gabe Morgan
Ricky Treon
Andrew Monroe
Elizabeth Williams

Jeremiah Cunningham
Niccole Caan
Dusty Boyd
Derek Porterfield
Mike Willbanks
Jim Livingston
Kaleb West
Kenny Nagunst
LaMyiah Harvel
Travis Tidmore
Beth Duke

ABOUT THE AUTHOR

Andrew J Brandt is a graduate of West Texas A&M University and the author of multiple bestsellers, including the #1 young adult thriller *The Treehouse.* In theory, he is writing his next novel. In reality, however, he is on the patio with a beer and watching the Chicago Cubs.

Andrew resides in Texas with his wife and children.

For more information, follow Andrew J Brandt on Facebook at facebook.com/writerbrandt or on Instagram at @writerbrandt.

Subscribe to his newsletter and purchase autographed paperback books and other products at his website www.writerbrandt.com.

CPSIA information can be obtained
at www.ICGtesting.com
Printed in the USA
FSHW011002101020
74566FS

9 781735 220604